stand there and
pretend nothing's wrong?'

'What are you talking about?'

'This.' Emily couldn't believe she was voluntarily pointing out her flaw.

'Oh, your birthmark? I see it. So what?'

'"So what?" he says. You could have given me a heads-up that I'd gone out in public like this.'

She didn't know why she was taking her mistake out on him, when he'd been nothing but supportive. But her lashing out might have had something to do with this being the most vulnerable she'd felt since arriving on the island.

'I assumed you were actually comfortable enough around us to stop hiding away.'

'You weren't shocked?'

'If I'm honest, I knew about it. But even if I hadn't it doesn't make any difference to me. Your birthmark is part of you. How could it be anything other than beautiful?'

He tilted her chin up so she had to look in his eyes and believe what she saw there—pure, undiluted desire.

Joe leaned forward and placed a light kiss on the exact spot between her cheek and her nose, where her greatest weakness blazed brightly. She held her breath. It was one of those moments she'd dreamed of, when someone would embrace her, warts and all, not shy away from any part of her. It was better than she'd ever imagined.

Dear Reader,

I'm a big fan of modern-day adventurers and those TV programmes in which they're dropped at remote locations with nothing but a camera and the will to survive. Mainly because I come from the 'What if?' school of thought, and prefer a cosy seat in my comfort zone to camping in the potentially spider-infested unknown. I admire that devil-may-care attitude to life—even though I watch those shows wondering why people would put themselves in unnecessary danger.

When ex-army doc Joe came to my mind he had that same adventurous spirit. He flits from one exciting escapade to another with no intention of settling down. Until he meets GP Emily, who is trying to break free from her own boring world, and begins to see the attraction in having someone to share his experiences with.

Although the remote island where they both arrive to volunteer their medical services is beautiful and welcoming, Emily's insecurities are in danger of stifling her enjoyment. Thank goodness Joe is there to give her a little nudge forward when she needs it.

Now I come to think about it, he kind of reminds me of my husband…

I do hope you enjoy going on Emily and Joe's exotic adventure with them. It was certainly fun to write!

Lots of love,

Karin xx

THE COURAGE TO LOVE HER ARMY DOC

BY
KARIN BAINE

Published in Great Britain 2016
By Mills & Boon, an imprint of HarperCollins*Publishers*
1 London Bridge Street, London, SE1 9GF

© 2016 Karin Baine

ISBN: 978-0-263-06554-1

Karin Baine lives in Northern Ireland with her husband, two sons, and her out-of-control notebook collection. Her mother's and her grandmother's vast collections of books inspired her love of reading and her dream of becoming a Mills & Boon author. Now she can tell people she has a *proper* job! You can follow Karin on Twitter, @karinbaine1, or visit her website for the latest news—karinbaine.com.

Books by Karin Baine

Mills & Boon Medical Romance

French Fling to Forever
A Kiss to Change Her Life
The Doctor's Forbidden Fling

Visit the Author Profile page
at millsandboon.co.uk for more titles.

For the ladies who've shared this adventure with me—
Ann, Cherie, Donna, Doris, Heather, Joanne, Julia,
June, Kiru, Michelle, Rima, Sharon, Stacy, Stephanie,
Sukhi, Summerita, Suzy, Tammy, Teresa and Xandra.
UCW was where it all began.

With thanks also to the residents of Los Balcones
and the members of 'The Monday Club'
who bring a little sunshine into my life.

And to George—the other half of me.

CHAPTER ONE

PARADISE. IT WAS the only word to describe these sun-drenched islands that Emily Clifford hoped were going to change her life. Unfortunately, she hadn't accounted for the distance she would have to travel to find her solace.

Travel sickness wasn't something she'd ever suffered before or she would've had one of her colleagues at the GP practice prescribe her something before she'd left England. If she'd been thinking clearly she might have realised that accessing one of these remote Fijian islands would take more than a taxi ride. Her first day after landing at the airport on the main island, Viti Levu, walking through the markets, and her night at a luxurious five-star resort now seemed a lifetime ago.

Today's white-knuckle charter flight, followed by a bone-jangling cross-country drive and hours of sailing these waters, had taken their toll.

The only thing she was looking forward to more than a shower and bed was seeing Peter, her stepbrother, waiting for her. He was the reason she was even attempting this adventure. The chance to prove her ex-husband wrong about her being *boring* was simply a bonus.

She and Greg had been together since high school, married for ten years, but it hadn't been enough. She hadn't been enough.

When Peter had told her about the mission out here and how they were struggling to find medical professionals to volunteer, she'd jumped at the chance to help for a while. Not least because this fortnight away meant she'd be occupied while Greg and Little Miss Bit-on-the-Side held the wedding of the year.

Another swell of nausea rose as the boat bobbed again but this had to be better than sitting at home, crying over her wedding photographs and wondering where it had all gone wrong.

As they finally reached the far side of the island and prepared to go ashore, she could see a figure sitting cross-legged at the water's edge. She waved manically, desperate more than ever to get off this boat and find comfort in the arms of her big brother.

With her hand shielding her eyes from the glaring sun, she squinted at her welcome party of one slowly getting to his feet. He appeared to have grown in the two years since she'd last seen him, and he was leaner than she remembered, as though someone had stretched him like golden-coloured toffee.

Eventually she had to come to terms with the fact that no amount of sand, sea and sun could cause such a physical transformation. Disappointment settled in her belly as she realised it wasn't Peter at all. She was going to have to wait for her tea and sympathy for a bit longer.

She'd done her best to be strong over this past year and a half, holding it together as she'd moved out of her marital home and keeping a smile in place for all her patients when she'd been dying inside. For a short time she wanted to stop pretending she wasn't crushed by the rejection and it didn't take every ounce of strength just to get out of bed in the morning and face the world. Ten minutes of being the baby sister, crying out her pain to her big bro, would help reset the factory settings. Two weeks doing what she loved, what she was qualified to do, would remind her she was more than a redundant wife. She'd lasted this long for a shoulder to cry on so waiting a few extra minutes wouldn't kill her. Although she couldn't swear the pent-up anger and emotion she'd been gearing up to release wouldn't seep out somewhere along the way.

Her bejewelled sandals and floral maxi-dress flapped through the water as she stepped ashore. In hindsight, it hadn't been the ideal choice of travelling outfit. Her feet ached, her dress was creased and as she came face-to-face with the hunk on the beach she was pretty sure the flower in her hair was wilting. What had been an attempt to get into the holiday spirit had probably succeeded in making her appear even more ridiculous than usual, like a stereotypical tourist instead of a qualified professional hoping to fit effortlessly into society.

With his close-cropped brown hair and dressed in mid-length khaki shorts and navy T-shirt, her greeter looked more action man than island native. There was no sign of a grass skirt anywhere. Unfortunately.

'Hi. I'm Emily.' She held out her hand for him to shake but he bypassed the traditional greeting to head for the boat. The bit of research she'd done said they mostly spoke English here on Yasi island but perhaps she'd found the one local who didn't.

He began unloading her luggage, muscles flexing as he hurled her case and boxes of supplies onto the white sand.

'Bula.' She tried again, using the one Fijian word she'd picked up on her travels so far.

The Peter impostor waved off her last link to civilisation and came back to join her.

'Bula to you too.' The cut-glass British accent didn't fit with the swarthy skin but the familiar tongue and the glimpse of a smile put her mind at ease about being stranded here with an uncommunicative stranger.

'You're English?'

'Yeah. From Oxford, actually. I'm Joe. Joe Braden.' This time he did shake her hand, the firm grip showing the strength behind those muscles.

Emily shivered, regardless of the tropical heat. Clearly she'd been on her own too long when a single handshake was enough to get her excited. Not that she was ready for the dating game. In the day and age when physical attributes held more value than loyalty or commitment, she was in no rush to put herself through any more heartache.

'Joe Braden... Why does that name ring a bell?' They'd never met. She'd have remembered if they had.

'I served with Peter in Afghanistan.' The smile disappeared as quickly as it had formed.

That made sense of the military haircut and the no-nonsense attitude. She'd heard that name in conversation and she was sure there was an extra nugget of information tied to it that was just out of reach in her subconscious.

'Where is he? No offence, but I had hoped he'd be here to meet me.' She didn't want to get into a conversation about their time in combat and she doubted he'd be keen to rehash the whole experience either. It had been hell for all those involved, including the families waiting anxiously at home for their safe return. Peter's decision to leave the army and begin a life dedicated to his faith had been a relief to everyone who loved him.

'None taken. We couldn't be sure exactly what time to expect you and Peter had a service this evening. I volunteered for lookout duty.' He handed her a suitcase and a holdall while he hoisted the large box onto his shoulder.

She didn't dare ask how long he'd waited. His lips, drawn into a thin line and his apparent hurry to get moving, told her it had probably been too long. Not exactly the welcome she'd been hoping for.

Joe was already taking great strides across the beach,

so Emily traipsed after him as fast as she could with a
holdall hooked over one shoulder and a suitcase in the
other, waddling like a colourful penguin. There was no
immediate sign of human habitation nearby and she didn't
relish the thought of being left behind.

'What brings you out here anyway?' She caught up
with him at the bottom of a steep, grassy slope. Their
journey apparently wasn't going to be an easy or short
one. Some small talk might help it pass quicker.

'Your stepbrother.'

'You're visiting Peter?' He hadn't mentioned having
company in his emails. She hadn't counted on sharing his
attention. As pitiful as that sounded, she hadn't seen him
in two whole years and wanted to make up for lost time.
Who knew where he'd be going next or how long he'd be
gone? Quality time with him wasn't going to be quite the
same with surly soldier dude tagging along.

'I'm here as a medical volunteer, the same as you. I'll
be here for another month. Maybe. I prefer to keep on the
move. What you would call a modern-day adventurer, I
guess. This is the longest I've actually spent in one place
since leaving the army, which is entirely down to your
stepbrother's powers of persuasion.' He didn't even slow
his pace to deliver the news, leaving her staring open-
mouthed at him.

There were two things wrong with that statement. First
of all, it meant he had personal intel on her already if he
knew why she was there. She didn't have her stepbrother
down as the gossipy type since he hadn't seen the need
to share information concerning her new companion, so
perhaps soldier boy had insisted on a debriefing before
meeting his assigned target. Goodness knew what went
on between ex-military buddies, they had a bro code mere
mortals could never infiltrate, but she hoped any discussion about her arrival hadn't included details of her failed

marriage. That shame was exactly what she was trying to escape.

Secondly, his introduction undoubtedly meant she'd be working alongside this man for the duration of her stay. Trying to get more than a few words out of him on this trek was proving hard enough.

In her version of this medical outreach programme she was simply transferring her cosy GP office to an exotic location without interference from third parties. Peter had sounded so delighted to hear she was coming she'd assumed she'd be the sole medical professional in residence. This Joe was stealing all her thunder.

'Do I call you Dr? Sergeant? Joe...?' She was going to have serious words with her stepbrother about dumping her on a complete stranger without a word of warning. It immediately put her on the back foot when Peter should have known how important it was for her to feel comfortable in her surroundings.

'Joe will do just fine.'

She couldn't work out if the reluctance to engage in conversation was personal or he was simply trying to conserve energy. The hike up this hill was a test of endurance in itself, never mind the heavy box he was balancing on his broad shoulders. She was starting to regret packing the weighty school books she'd brought with her as a gift.

'Isn't there someone who could give us a hand?' She was tired, achy and full of guilt, watching him shift the burden from one shoulder to the other.

'Did you bring the *yaqona*?' He ignored her question to stop and ask one of his own, as if hers wasn't important enough to deserve the few seconds it would take to answer it. With any luck this place was big enough to house two independent clinics. There was no way she was spending the duration of this trip with someone so rude.

'Yes. It's in this bag.' She, however, was polite enough

to answer him. Peter had at least given her the heads up about bringing gifts with her, including the root of this pepper plant. Apparently it was some sort of payment for her stay among the villagers, even though it did look kind of funky to her. She would have preferred to give him a pot plant or a nice bottle of wine with a thank-you card.

'Good. We'll go and make *sevusevu* now with the chief.'

'Can't we do that later? I really need to shower and freshen up.' By the time they reached their destination she wouldn't be fit to be seen in public.

'No can do. You have to show your respect to the tribal leader before you can integrate yourself into village life. If you respect the customs here it'll ensure you become part of the community.'

Right now, the heat and humidity were making her feel as though her face was melting. She was very wary of her potentially sliding make-up and the fact he was telling her she wouldn't get the chance to redo it. The heavy, thick concealer she wore to cover her birthmark was the one essential from home she couldn't do without.

She was self-conscious of the deep red port wine stain dominating the left side of her face, so noticeable against her otherwise pale skin. It was something that had caused her a great deal of distress over the years. And not only from uneducated, tactless strangers. Her own mother had been ashamed of her appearance. She'd told her that when she'd forced her through painful, ineffective laser treatment as a child. She'd shown it when she'd left the family home without her. In the end it had been the camouflage make-up and the love of her father's new family that had helped her live with it.

This was a big ask for her anyway, to come to foreign lands alone, never mind leaving herself exposed and open to scrutiny from strangers.

As they crested the hill she could see the settlement nestled below. It was now or never.

She stopped and dropped her bags. This trip was always going to be about improvising and making use of whatever resources she had at the time.

'What are you doing?' Joe raised an eyebrow at her as she rooted through her belongings for her mirror compact.

'I need to look my best if I'm going to meet someone of such great importance.' She made a few repairs before she scared small children and animals, ignoring Joe's shake of the head.

'You know, that's really not necessary. You should let your skin breathe and I'm sure you look just as amazing without it.'

There was no time to linger on the fact he'd paid her a compliment as he spun on his heel and started walking again. Besides, he'd be running if he knew what really lay beneath. She took one last glance in the mirror to check for any errant red patches shining through the layers of powder and paint and packed her precious cargo away again to follow him. Now she'd had a chance to boost her confidence again she could face any new challenge.

Joe couldn't hang about to watch her plaster that stuff over her face. He knew why she did it, of course, he'd seen the photographs of his kid sister Peter had kept with him out in Afghanistan. It simply irked him that someone had made her feel as though she had to use it to keep her real self from view. He knew how it was to have people devalue your worth so readily over a minor flaw.

Okay, his hearing had taken a hit along with the rest of him on the front line but that didn't mean he should have been written off altogether. The army might think all he was good for now was a desk job or teaching but he had no intention of sitting still. Fiji was just one stop on the list of adventures he'd embarked on since taking medical retirement.

According to Peter, Emily had had a rough time of it lately but Joe knew how empowering these trips abroad could be. His time trekking in Nepal, island hopping in the Philippines and swimming on the Great Barrier Reef had kept him from focusing on all the negatives in his past. With any luck she'd return at the end of this mission equally as upbeat, not caring a jot about other people's perceptions of her.

Although how she could think she was anything other than stunning he didn't know. The second she'd stepped ashore he'd known he was in trouble.

His decision to volunteer as official island greeter had been born of curiosity. He'd seen the worn photographs of her and Peter as kids, the shy Emily always hiding behind her stepbrother, and he'd wondered about the woman she'd become. The doctor he was going to be working alongside for the foreseeable future.

In the four weeks he'd already spent in this island paradise she was the most beautiful sight he'd seen yet. With the golden waves of her hair shining in the sunlight, her turquoise eyes the colour of the water and her slender form draped in azure, she could've stepped out of a shampoo advert. It was too bad she was his mate's little sister and nursing a broken heart. Two things that immediately put her off limits. Even if hearing-impaired ex-army docs were her thing.

He'd let enough of his army buddies down without failing Peter too. Neither was he in the market for any sort of emotional entanglements. Emily was literally carrying more baggage than he was prepared to take on. He was more of a backpacking guy, travelling light with no intention of setting down roots. Although he helped out with these outreach programmes now and then when people were in dire need, he was better off on his own. It meant no long-term responsibility to anyone but himself.

The last time he'd been charged with the welfare of people close to him, it had cost two of his colleagues their lives. When the IED had knocked him to kingdom come he'd failed to be there for the men he'd had a duty of care for. Next to the young families left without fathers, his loss seemed insignificant. These days he preferred to keep his wits about him rather than become too complacent and safe in his surroundings.

'Are we there yet?' Emily was smiling as she jogged to keep up with him.

At least when she was close he could hear her or interpret her facial expressions. He only had a six per cent loss of hearing but sometimes it meant he missed full conversations going on in the background. More often than not he chose to let people think he was an arrogant sod over revealing his weakness. He and Emily had their pride in common.

'Very nearly. Now, there are a few protocols to be aware of before presenting the *yaqona* for the kava ceremony. You're dressed modestly enough so that shouldn't be a problem.' He took the opportunity for a more in-depth study of her form, though he wasn't likely to forget in a hurry how she looked today.

'What's the kava ceremony?' She eyed him suspiciously, as if he might be luring her to the village as some sort of human sacrifice.

'Basically, it's a welcoming ceremony with the most senior tribal members present. They grind the *yaqona*, or kava, and make it into a drink for you to take with them in a traditional ceremony. All visitors are invited to take part when they first arrive on the island.'

'It's not one of those hallucinogenic substances you hear about, is it? I don't want to be seeing fairies dancing about all night in front of my eyes. I'm not even a big drinker because I don't enjoy that feeling of being out of control.' She was starting to get herself into a flap for no reason.

Joe hadn't even asked questions when he'd taken part in his first kava ceremony, he'd just gone with the flow. He embraced every new experience with gusto, whereas Emily seemed to fear it.

'Don't worry. It's nothing sinister, although the taste leaves a lot to be desired. There shouldn't be any fairy visions keeping you awake. If anything, it's known to aid sleep, among other things.' He kept the claims of its aphrodisiac properties to himself rather than freak her out any further.

'I don't think that's something I'm going to have a problem with tonight.' She set her case down and rubbed her palms on her dress before lifting it again. The heavy labour in less-than-ideal circumstances was something she was going to have to get used to and only time would tell if she was up to it.

He, on the other hand, had a feeling his peace of mind here had suddenly been thrown into chaos.

It was just as well he thrived on a challenge.

CHAPTER TWO

ALL EMILY WANTED was a familiar face and familiar things around her. It wasn't a lot to ask for and the sooner she got her bags unpacked and her clinic in the sun set up the better. Then she might be able to finally relax. She'd had all the excitement she needed just getting here.

Her pulse skittered faster as the ramshackle buildings with their corrugated-iron roofs came into view. This was as far from her humdrum life as she could get and a definite two-fingered salute to her ex.

'Can I refuse to take part in this kava thing?' She'd used up her quota of bravery already. Drinking unknown substances with strangers was the sort of thing that could make her the subject of one of those 'disappearances unsolved' programmes.

Her idea of living dangerously was putting an extra spoonful of sugar in her cuppa at bedtime, not imbibing a local brew of origin unknown to her. It wasn't that she'd heard anything but good things about these people, she was just scared of all this *newness*. This would've been so much easier if Peter was here with her instead of the scowling Joe.

'You have free will, of course you can refuse. It would, however, show a distinct lack of respect for your hosts.'

That would be a no, then. It was going to be difficult

enough fitting in here, without incurring the wrath of the community from the get-go.

Trust and respect were vital components between a doctor and her patients. It had taken her a long time to gain both from her colleagues and the locals when she'd first joined the GP practice at home. Only years of hard work, building her reputation, had moved her from being last option to first choice for her patients.

With only two weeks to re-create that success here she'd have to take every opportunity available to ingratiate herself. Even if she was breaking out in a cold sweat at what that meant she could be walking into.

They passed a white building, larger than the rest, which her tour guide informed her was the village school. Although lessons were surely over for the day, the children were congregated on the patch of green surrounding it, playing ball games. There was a chorus of '*Bula!*' as the youngsters waved in their direction.

Unfortunately, one boy by the volleyball net was too distracted by their arrival to see the ball coming straight for him. The loud smack as it connected full in his face even made Emily flinch. As the child crumpled to the ground, for a split second she wondered if there was some sort of protocol she should follow as she hadn't been officially introduced. Common sense quickly overrode her worry and she dropped her bags to run to him. It was only when she was battling through the throng of children to reach him that she realised Joe had followed too. They knelt on either side of the boy, who was thankfully still conscious but clearly winded.

'If you could just stay still for us, sweetheart, we want to give you a check over. That was quite a hit you took there.' She couldn't see any blood or bruising as yet but she wanted him to stay flat until they'd given him a quick examination.

'Hi, Joni. This is Emily, the new doctor. You know, Pastor Peter's sister?' Joe made the introduction she'd omitted to do herself, and was already checking the boy's pupils with a small torch he'd retrieved from one of his pockets.

She'd bet her life he had a Swiss Army knife and a compass somewhere in those cargo shorts too. He was the type of guy who was always prepared, like a rugged, muscly Boy Scout. The only survival essentials she carried were make-up, teabags and chocolate biscuits, none of which were particularly useful at present. The few medical supplies she had with her were packed somewhere in her abandoned luggage.

Life as an island doctor certainly wasn't going to run to the office hours she was used to. She was going to be permanently on call and if she didn't come equipped, deferring to her army medic colleague was going to become the norm. That feeling of inadequacy could defeat the purpose of her personal journey here if she didn't get with the programme. This trip was primarily to bring medical relief to the people of the island and she could do without uncovering any new flaws to obsess over.

'Do you know where you are, Joni? Or what happened?' She wrestled back some control, determined not to let the issue of a pocket torch spiral into a major meltdown in her neurotic brain.

That earned her an *Are you serious?* glare. 'I'm lying on the ground because you two won't let me get up after I got hit in the face with a ball.'

Joe snickered as she was educated by her first patient.

'Dr Emily's making sure the bump on the head hasn't caused any serious damage, smart guy.' He ruffled the boy's hair, clearly already acquainted with the child.

She figured he was using her first name to break the

ice a little because she was a stranger. Either that or he didn't know what surname she was currently going under.

It was a subject she hadn't fully resolved herself. Greg Clifford was going to be someone else's husband soon. She no longer had any claim over his name, or anything else. Yet reverting back to her maiden name of Jackson was confirmation that her marriage had failed. She'd been returned unwanted for a second time, like a mangy stray dog. The idea of going back on the singles market felt very much like waiting for someone to take pity on her and find her a forever home.

She tried to refocus her attention back from her ex to the present. He didn't deserve any more of her time since all the years she'd given him had apparently meant so little.

'Do you have any pain in your neck?'

Her choice of words had her patient sniggering at her again.

'Come on, Joni. We're trying to help you here. We need to know if you're hurting anywhere before we get you back on your feet.'

It was comforting to find Joe had her back this time, even if his apparent seniority here was irksome.

'I'm okay.' As if to try to prove their fears unwarranted, Joni jumped to his feet, only to have to reach out and steady himself by grabbing Joe's arm.

If Emily was honest, she'd have made a grab for the strong and sturdy desert island doc too in similar circumstances.

'Really?' Joe arched a dark eyebrow as he glanced down at his new small-child accessory.

Joni shrugged but made no further wisecracks.

'We should really get him checked out properly.' Although he bore no immediate signs of concussion, it didn't mean they should rule it out altogether.

As well as getting a cold compress to prevent swelling, she'd prefer to keep him under observation in case of headaches or vomiting. He'd taken quite a wallop and although the skull was there to protect the brain there was always a chance the knock could cause the brain to swell or bleed. She didn't like taking unnecessary chances.

'The best option for now is to get him to Miriama's.' Joe crouched down for the patient to jump on his back. A piggyback was apparently the equivalent of an ambulance around here.

'Isn't there a medical centre we can take him to?' A small bird of panic fluttered its wings in her chest. She'd been led to believe there'd be some sort of facility for her to practise from. He might be used to treating people in the field but she certainly wasn't.

'Of sorts, but Miriama is his grandmother and the closest thing they have to a medic. She can keep an eye on him until you make *sevusevu* and if his condition changes we'll only be a few minutes away.'

It didn't slip her attention that he intended coming with her. In the absence of her brother she supposed he was going to have to do as backup. At least this incident showed he could be a calming influence when the need arose and she trusted he would keep her grounded until she tracked down her sibling.

'What about my things?' As they followed the dirt trail further into the village she fretted over her worldly possessions abandoned on the hillside.

'No one's going to steal them. We'll come back for the *yaqona* and send someone to take the rest back to Miriama's later.' He strode on ahead, unconcerned with her petty worries or the weight strapped around his neck.

She could picture him in his army gear, bravely heading into battle with his kit on his back, and it gave her chills. The idea of her brother in a war zone had always freaked her out and there'd been no greater relief than when he'd left the army. She was glad he was no longer in danger. Joe too. Life here might be more unconventional than she was used to but she didn't have to worry about anyone getting shot or blown up.

With her imagination slowing her down, she was forced to run and catch up again. The sandals slapping against her bare feet really weren't suitable footwear for chasing fit men in a hurry.

'Why should my luggage end up at Miriama's?' That obscure snippet of information hadn't passed her by.

'That's where you're going to be staying for the next fortnight. Miriama's your host.'

Although she hadn't expected the luxury of last night's five-star resort, she'd imagined she'd be staying with her brother rather than another stranger.

'Peter's staying with the village chief. He's earned a great deal of respect from the community for his endeavours here.' Joe headed off her next question before she could ask it. She couldn't help but wonder what his own arrangements were.

'And you? Where do you lay your head at night?' Only when the words left her lips did she realise how nosy that sounded. She hadn't intended prying into his personal life but this was all new to her. She didn't know if he was presented with pretty young virgins and his own house to thank him for his services. It would certainly explain her brother's reluctance to leave the village.

He cocked his head to one side, his mouth twitching as he fought a smile. 'Well, there's a new arrival in my bed tonight—'

She held her hand up before he went into graphic detail. 'I shouldn't have asked. It's none of my business.'

'So I'm moving from Miriama's into the clinic.'

It took a second for the image of Joe cavorting with exotic beauties to clear and let his words sink in.

'I'm taking your bed? Honestly, that's not necessary. I'm more than willing to take your place at the clinic.' She didn't know what that entailed but she'd take it over the lack of privacy in someone else's house.

Joe shook his head. 'The clinic's a glorified hut with two camp beds and a supply cupboard. You'll find no comfort there. I, on the other hand, am used to kipping in ditches, or worse. It's no hardship for me. Besides, you'll be doing me a favour.' He gave a furtive glance back at his charge to make sure he wasn't listening. 'I don't want to offend Miriama but I prefer the peace and quiet of being alone. I'm not used to domesticity.'

Perhaps it was because he was the first man to get so close to her in well over a year or the picture he painted of himself as some wild creature who couldn't be tamed but the shivers were back, causing havoc along her spine and the back of her neck.

Okay, she wasn't happy with the arrangements made on her behalf but she couldn't deny him his bed choice when he'd gone so far out of his way for her already. She couldn't form a logical argument anyway when her brain was still stuck on a freeze frame of caveman Joe.

The smiling Miriama was as welcoming as anyone could hope for. Until she found out Emily had yet to meet with the tribal elders and shooed them both back out of the door. She'd unhitched her grandson with the promise of getting some ice for the bump on his forehead and accepted some paracetamol, which Joe had produced from his shorts of many pockets. This new informal approach to treatment would take some getting used to. Just like her new co-worker would.

They retrieved her gifts for the community on the way

back to the chief's house and dispatched the rest of her belongings back to her temporary lodgings with the children. Trust didn't come easily to her any more but she was willing to take a leap of faith safe in the knowledge there were few places on the island to hide. She'd found that out the minute she'd set foot on the beach.

Now she was standing on the doorstep of the most important man on Yasi as Joe entered into a dialogue she assumed involved her arrival. It was hard to tell because they were conversing in Fijian, another skill he'd apparently acquired in his short time here and one more advantage over her. Languages had never been her strong point. Along with keeping a husband.

She was hanging back as the menfolk discussed her business, still hoping for a way out, when a hand clamped down on her shoulder.

'Hey, sis. Long time no see.'

In her desire to be accepted she thought she'd imagined her stepbrother standing beside her in a garish pink hibiscus shirt but there was no mistaking the bear hug as anything but the real deal as the breath was almost squeezed out of her.

'Peter?' The tears were already welling in her eyes with relief to have finally found some comfort.

'I wouldn't miss this for the world. Now, Joe will be acting as our "chief" since he's the eldest of our group, or temporary tribe. It's his job to present the kava root to the elders. We'll talk you through everything else once we're inside.'

He instructed her to remove her sandals before they entered. Sandwiched between her brother and Joe was the safest she'd felt in an age. They sat down on woven mats strewn across the floor of the main room, surrounded by those she assumed were the elders of the village.

'I take it everything met with their approval?' She

leaned over to whisper to her unofficial leader sitting cross-legged beside her.

Joe kept his gaze straight ahead, completely ignoring her. She didn't know if pretending she didn't exist was part of the process until she was accepted into the community or if he was completely relinquishing all responsibility for her now Peter had appeared. Either way, it hurt.

She leaned back the other direction toward Peter. 'Am I persona non grata around here until the ceremony's over?'

He frowned at her. 'What makes you say that?'

She nodded at her silent partner. 'Your friend here can be a little cold when he wants. Thanks for landing me with a complete stranger, by the way. Just what I needed to make me feel at home. Not.'

The cheesy grin told her he'd done it on purpose. 'I thought you two could do with some team bonding since you'll be working together, and he volunteered in the first place. I should probably mention he's a bit hard of hearing, especially if you're whispering.'

'I had no idea!' Shame enveloped her. It had never entered her head that hearing impairment could've been an issue with Joe when he was so young and capable. She of all people should've known not to make assumptions based on people's appearances.

'Yeah. IED blast. The one where we lost Ste and Batesy.'

The pieces she'd been scrambling to put together slowly fitted into place. Of course, she'd heard of Sergeant Joe Braden. He'd been one of Peter's best friends and that blast had made her brother finally experience for himself the worry and fear of losing someone close. It hadn't been long after that he'd made the decision to change his career path completely. She hated it that his friends had suffered so much for him to reach that point and now she'd met the man behind the name, that blast held more significance than ever.

She sneaked a sideways peek at him. His strong profile gave no clue to his impairment. There was no physical evidence to provoke a discussion or sympathy. Unlike her, whose scars were there for the world to see and pass judgement on.

Over the years she'd heard all sorts of theories whispered behind her back. From being scalded as a baby to being the victim of a house fire or an acid attack, she'd heard them all. In the end it had been easier to simply cover the birthmark than to endure the constant rumours.

Joe came across as a stronger, more confident person than she could ever hope to be, but that kind of injury must've caused him the same level of anguish at one time or another. Someone like him would've seen it as a personal weakness when their whole career had been built on personal fitness and being the best. She barely knew him but she could tell that the word 'courage' was stamped all over his DNA. She was even more in awe of him now she knew something of his past.

As though he could sense her staring at the sharp lines of his jaw and the soft contours of his lips, Joe slowly turned to face her. 'There's a certain guide to drinking kava. You clap once with a cupped hand, making a hollow sound, and yell, '*Bula!*' Drink it in one gulp, clap three times and say, '*Mathe*.' You'll be offered the option of high tide or low tide. I strongly advise low tide for your first time.'

'Okay…' She might've put this down as some sort of elaborate practical joke if it wasn't for the twinkle in his eye and his excited-puppy enthusiasm while waiting for the ceremony to begin. In contrast to her reservations about the whole palaver, he clearly relished being a part of the culture.

He fell silent again as the villagers began to grind up the kava in the centre of the room. There were few women present but as the proceedings got under way she didn't feel intimidated at all. The relaxed atmosphere and the men playing guitar in the corner of the room gave it more of a party vibe. Despite her initial reservations, she was actually beginning to relax.

After they ground the kava, it was strained through a cloth bag into a large wooden bowl. It looked like muddy water to her but the chief drank it down without hesitation, as did Peter and Joe. She was thankful for the advice when it came to her turn. Requesting 'low tide' ensured the coconut shell she was offered was only half-full.

It didn't taste any better than it looked. Like mud. Bitter, peppery mud. Definitely an acquired taste but she drank it in one gulp and did the happy, clappy thing which seemed to please everyone. For unknown reasons the proud look from Joe was the one that gave her tingles.

In fact, it wasn't long before her mouth and tongue seemed to go completely numb.

'Whath happenin'?' she lisped to Peter as her tongue suddenly seemed to be too big for her mouth.

'That'll be the kava kicking in. It's a very mild narcotic but don't worry, it'll pass soon.' Something that wasn't bothering her God-fearing brother as he accepted another bowl.

She declined to partake in any further rounds, which her hosts accepted without any offence. Clearly she'd already proved herself as a worthy guest. Thank goodness. Any more and she'd either pass out or lose control of the rest of her faculties. All she wanted now was for Joe to take her to bed. Home. She meant home...

Joe had become accustomed to the bitter-tasting celebration drink to the point even a second bowl had had no effect. He was aware, however, that it might not be the same for Emily, especially as she was probably tired and hungry and currently running her fingertips across her lips. Numb no doubt from the small taste she'd had. He watched as she darted her tongue out to lick them, drawing his attention and thoughts to where they shouldn't go.

Emily was his best friend's sister and obviously running away from her demons to have come somewhere so clearly out of her comfort zone. She wasn't, and couldn't ever be, someone he could hook up with. Normally he didn't hesitate to act on his attraction to women on his travels. Life was too short and so was his stay in their company when he was always on the move. This was an entirely different situation. Peter would always be part of his life and he wouldn't jeopardise that friendship when he invariably moved on. There was no point thinking of her as anything other than a hindrance, a soft soul who'd probably never left her cosy office and would only get in his way. A liability he didn't want or need.

Now she had been fully accepted into the community the villagers soon let their curiosity shine through and asked the questions he already knew the answers to.

'Do you have a husband?'

'What about children?'

The first question had thrown her, he could see it in her wide aquamarine eyes and knew why. Peter had confided in him about her marital problems long before her arrival because he'd worried how she might've been affected by it all. He'd taken her acceptance to help out on the mission as the first step to her recovery and had sworn Joe to secrecy. Not that it was any of his business anyway and he'd no wish to embarrass her by answering for her now. This was her call.

She took her time in finding an answer she was happy to give them. 'No husband or children.'

It didn't surprise him to find her divorce wasn't a subject she intended to discuss. She wasn't the only one who preferred to keep private matters out of the public domain. Only Peter knew about his past in the army and the fallout from the IED, and that's the way it would stay. Much like Emily, he'd decided he didn't need sympathy or pitying looks.

The gathering and the kava seemed to relax her more as the evening wore on, and she fielded their questions about her work without giving away too much personal information. A single, female doctor was something of a novelty out here and he understood their fascination. He was caught up in it too.

As usual, the evening ended with music and dancing, with both he and a yawning Emily watching from the sidelines.

'You can go any time you're ready.'

'Really? They won't mind?' In contrast to her earlier attempt to cry off from proceedings, she now seemed apprehensive about potentially upsetting her hosts. That was the beauty of the people here. They were so warm and friendly it was impossible to feel like an outsider for too long.

'Sure. You've done everything right and they'll understand you're tired. This could go on all night.' He got up and helped her to her feet.

'Peter?' She waited for her brother to join her but he wasn't as ready as his companions to leave.

Joe couldn't wait for some time out from the crowd. Sometimes the white noise could be a bit overwhelming when he couldn't pick out individual conversations.

'You could see Emily to Miriama's, couldn't you? It's on the way back to the medical centre.'

He couldn't fault Peter's logic since he was staying with the chief anyway but it meant prolonging his role as escort a while longer. This was beyond the remit of his volunteer medic/best friend duties and he didn't want it to become a habit. He'd only known Emily a few hours and for someone who considered himself a lone wolf he'd already taken on too much responsibility.

'Fine.' He sighed with just enough sulkiness to let Peter know he wasn't happy playing babysitter any more.

The only thoughts in his head about Emily should be to do with the clinic and how they were going to make it work together. Now there was no chance of forgetting how beautiful she'd looked, sitting cross-legged, utterly transfixed with island life, if she was going to be the last thing he saw before going to sleep.

CHAPTER THREE

EMILY WAS STILL trying to shuffle back into her shoes as she trailed after Joe. If it wasn't for it being completely pitch-black outside without the streetlights she took for granted back home and the sense of direction that meant she shouldn't be allowed out of the house unsupervised, she'd totally have made her own way back without him. Joe's term as 'leader' had clearly ended given his reluctance to see her home. Not that she blamed him. She'd imposed long enough and as soon as she had five minutes alone with her brother she'd tear strips off him for palming her off on him all night.

Peter should have understood what a big deal it had been for her to come here and gone out of his way to look after her. She needed some TLC after everything she'd gone through, not being frog-marched home as if she'd broken curfew. This was supposed to build her confidence, not reaffirm that idea she spoiled everyone's fun.

'I'm sorry you've copped babysitting duties for the nuisance little sister again.' She made sure she spoke loudly and clearly for him to hear. She didn't know the full extent of his hearing loss. He wasn't wearing a hearing aid but he was the type of guy who wouldn't be seen with one even if he needed it.

'No problem. We can't have you stumbling about here

alone in the dark. It'll take a while for you to get your bearings but you'll be able to walk this island with your eyes shut in no time.'

She didn't correct him by admitting another of her weaknesses since he was probably pinning his hopes on it so he wouldn't have to do this again. However, without her chatter, the sound of his heavy footsteps dominated the night, reminding her he was trying to ditch her as soon as possible.

'So what was with all the questions back there? They're not planning on marrying me off to the chief's son, are they?' It was a pseudo-concern in an attempt at small talk. Mostly.

The footsteps stopped and she could hear him grinding the dirt underfoot as he spun round.

'You've watched way too many movies. These people are no different from you or me. They simply have a sense of tradition. They've accepted you as one of their own, there's no ulterior motive.'

She was caught so off balance by his passion as he spoke of his new friends that she stumbled. She made a grab for him in the dark to steady herself and found a nice sturdy bicep beneath her fingers.

'Sorry,' she mumbled, eventually letting go once the shock of coming into contact with bare male body parts wore off. Or at least when she thought the prolonged touching was entering the awkward and desperate phase. He may be lean but he was one hundred per cent solid hunk.

She was nodding her head and apologising as he defended his friends, in an attempt at a mature response, which probably shouldn't include going back for another squeeze.

'You're right. I…er…was thrown by the level of attention. I'm not used to it.' If anything she tried to avoid those kinds of situations where she was the focal point of interest in case people studied her too closely and spotted her secret shame.

She caught the glint of his smile in the moonlight as he looked down at her. Compared to her last port of call, she should've been more at ease under the cover of darkness but her birthmark may as well have been blazing under his night vision she felt so exposed here with him.

'You're beautiful and smart. Of course they want to know your story.' The tone of his voice was soft enough to snuggle into, never mind the unexpected compliment almost bringing her to a swoon.

Except he was back on the move again, not lingering for a romantic smooch under the stars. She definitely watched too many movies. Probably because reality was too damn anticlimactic. She sighed, forced to gather herself together and remember this was no holiday romance, as much as she wanted to get carried away as far from real life as possible.

He didn't elaborate on what had prompted the ego boost and she had to hold her tongue to stop herself from pushing for more praise. How had he reached the conclusion she was either of those things? And did he have any interest in her beyond work and doing favours for her brother? Would it matter if he did?

The resulting silence between them stretched out to Miriama's house, giving her time to get her head back out of the clouds. He hadn't seen her true, vivid, scarlet colours. His assessment of her looks and personality was based on a lie. He knew nothing of the scarred woman beneath who'd been rejected time and time again.

By the time they reached her doorstep she'd firmly landed her backside back on earth with a thud. All he'd been trying to do was illustrate how ridiculous her assumptions had been. He probably hadn't even meant what he'd said but it had been so long since a man had paid her a compliment she'd taken it and twisted it into something it wasn't. She blamed the kava. Apart from the numbness and the tingles, she'd add delusions to the list of side effects. She'd have to remember to ship a crate of the stuff back to England with her.

To Joe, the short walk to Miriama's seemed twice as long as usual. That was the trouble with island life. It was too easy to get caught up in the beauty of the surroundings. They should really think about investing in some streetlights here. The electric hum and fluorescent orange glare might have made this feel less like a walk home after a first date than the moonlight and the sound of the sea.

All he'd intended to do was put her mind at ease that the people here weren't perhaps as…duplicitous as those she may have encountered recently. Instead, those careless few words had given away his less-than-platonic thoughts about having her here. Now he was watching her in the dim light of the doorway, pouting and tracing the outline of her lips with her fingertips.

'What are you doing?' He cocked his head to one side, fixated by her fascinating courtship display. If this was designed to pique his interest even further, it was working. His whole body was standing to attention as he followed the soft lines of her mouth, envying the manicured nail that got to touch them.

'Just checking my lips are still there since I can't feel them any more.' She poked her pink tongue out, parting her lips to dampen them, leaving them moist and a temptation too great to ignore any longer.

He stepped forward to give her a soft peck on the lips. Enough to satisfy his curiosity but insufficient to quell the rising swell of desire inside.

If he didn't break away soon this would change from

a simple goodnight kiss into something steamier and liable to offend Miriama. Especially as Emily wasn't protesting against this.

'Yup. They're still there. Goodnight, Emily.' He turned his back on her and walked away so he couldn't see the dazed look in her eyes and her still-parted lips, although the sight and taste of her would probably be seared in his brain forever.

He ditched all thoughts of going to bed and chose the path back down to the beach instead. There was no point trying to go to sleep when adrenaline was pulsing through his whole body. That had been a dumb move, an impulsive one, one born of pure instinct and lack of judgement. He'd wanted to kiss her so he had, without any thought to the consequences of his actions. That spur-of-the-moment thinking was fine when it came to picking a new place to visit where no one but him would come a cropper if he made the wrong decision. When it came to kissing emotionally fragile divorcees related to his best friend it had the potential to get messy.

He lifted a pebble from the beach and threw it, watching it skim the surface of the water before disappearing into the darkness along with his common sense. He pitched another and another, venting his anger at himself in the only way possible without punching something. In the end he stripped off his clothes and chucked himself into the sea to cool off. Late-night skinny-dipping had often been a way for him to unwind but tonight it was his attempt to cleanse himself of his transgression. He didn't kiss women because he'd made an emotional connection with them, he kissed them because he wanted to. This was a woman he was going to be working with closely for the next two weeks and he was in serious trouble if he couldn't go one evening without controlling himself around her.

He dipped his head below the surface but even as he scrubbed his face with his hands he knew the cold salty water couldn't wipe away the taste and feel of her lips on his. The damage was already done. All he could do now was add it to the list of mistakes he carried with him and hope Emily didn't expect anything more from him than medical input and local knowledge. He'd hate to disappoint her as well as himself.

Emily suspected the local brew had a lot to do with her falling asleep the minute her head touched the pillow and the weird dreams that followed. She spent the night imagining she was stranded on a desert island with a hunky sea captain who looked suspiciously like Sgt Joe Braden coming to her rescue. There was no need to overanalyse it. It was simply her mind trying to make sense of the day's events, and better than spending all night worrying about what sort of creatures lurked in her small room, or thinking about that kiss.

Joe more than likely left dazed women in his wake with his throwaway kisses every day and would have no clue of the impact it had made on her. It was silly really to obsess over something so fleeting, but up until last night her husband had been the only man she'd ever kissed.

She remembered every tiny detail of the brief connection between her and Joe. The firm but tender pressure of his mouth on hers, the bitter taste of kava lingering on his lips and her body frozen while her veins burned with fire.

The past eighteen months had made her a jaded divorcee so she shouldn't have had her head turned so easily. She really needed to work on building up those walls if she was being a fangirl over a peck on the lips from a glorified babysitter.

Today was the start of her placement alongside last night's fantasy figure. There was no room for schoolgirl crushes when she was already on edge about working here. She'd risen with the sun, showered with the aid of a bucket of cold water, breakfasted on bread and jam with Miriama, and checked on Joni, but she couldn't put it off any longer. As she walked towards the medical centre she tried to focus on the positives instead of the nerves bundling in her stomach.

The sky was the brightest blue she'd ever seen, her skin was warmed by the sun and she'd swapped her usual restrictive formal attire for a strappy pink sundress and flats. She was confident in her work and her capabilities, it was more the personal aspects causing her anxieties. Last night she'd mixed well with the community but that had been in an informal setting. It hadn't escaped her attention that very few women had been present at the kava ceremony and they'd had to wait until the men had taken their fill before they'd been served. She hoped it was another nod to tradition rather than any prejudiced attitude towards women's role in society.

Joni had shown her the route back to the medical centre on his way to school and it really was nothing more than a glorified hut on the edge of the village. Thankfully the boy had shown no signs of concussion this morning but in her line of work it was always better to be safe than sorry when it could mean the difference between life and death. It was a shame that same adage had caused the end of her marriage. Playing it safe in her personal life had driven Greg away and made her sorrier than ever for the risks she hadn't taken.

Still, her love life, or lack of it, wasn't the sole reason she'd come all this way. Joe Braden certainly wasn't the risk she wanted to start with. She was here to help a community that didn't have immediate access to medical facilities, nothing more.

Once she set foot inside the designated workspace she

realised how difficult it was going to be to avoid further close contact with him.

'Welcome to your new clinic, Dr Emily.' A grinning Joe greeted her, his outstretched arms almost touching both sides of the hut.

The sun shone in behind him through the one window in the room, the rays outlining the tantalising V-shape of his torso through his loose white cotton shirt.

'You've got to be kidding.' She hadn't meant to vocalise her thoughts and for a shameful second she wished this was one time he hadn't heard her. No such luck.

'Hey, we gotta work with what we've got. I know you're used to all the mod cons at your practice but you have to remember the context here. Me, you and this equipment donated by the church is more than these people usually have.'

The good news was he thought her only concern was her new working conditions. The bad news was…her new working conditions.

There were two basic camp beds, not unlike the one she'd been put up in at Miriama's, a couple of medical storage lockers and chairs, some old IV stands and monitors and some sort of curtain on wheels she guessed was supposed to be a privacy screen. There were adequate facilities for routine health checks and not much else but enough to divide the workload and shared space.

'I think this will work best if we treat this as two different clinics and double the output. You do your thing and I'll do mine.' Never the twain to meet and make body contact ever again.

She moved one medical trolley to one side of the room and claimed her half by wheeling the screen between the two beds.

'If you say so…' Joe didn't sound convinced but at least he wasn't getting precious about this being his ter-

ritory. Chances were he was happy to block her out anyway after being forced to lead her around by the hand all
day yesterday.

'I do. This is going to work.' This new set-up enabled
her to take back some control of her life here and already
made her feel less nauseous about the days ahead.

This was never going to work. Joe had been here long
enough to understand the logistical nightmare of putting
her idea into practice. There simply wasn't enough room
to create two viable working spaces, although he didn't
try to dissuade her from attempting it. She'd work it out
for herself eventually without him coming across as a
tyrant by refusing to cooperate with her plans. It was his
fault she felt the need to put a barrier between them in
the first place.

After his antics last night he was lucky Peter hadn't
rounded up a posse to turf him off the island for laying
lips on his sister. He'd been beating himself up over it all
night and this display of skittish behaviour wasn't easing
his conscience at all. By all accounts Emily was recovering from an acrimonious split and definitely wasn't the
sort of woman he should be kissing on a whim.

His one saving grace was their apparent mutual decision not to mention it. Perhaps his casual walk away
had lessened the significance of the event. He might start
kissing everyone goodbye and make it out to be more of a
personal custom rather than the result of his attraction to
her. Although there was something intimate about seeing
her fuss around the bed where he'd been lying, thinking
about her, last night.

He'd been honest when he'd said he preferred the quiet
out here to Miriama's busy household. There was also
the added benefit of being able to see the door from his
bed. Combat had made him hypervigilant about his sur-

roundings. He wasn't comfortable in a room where he couldn't see all entry points. Army life taught a man that concealed entrances were all potential ambushes where the enemy could attack. That level of paranoia had been essential in his survival but it hadn't left him even after his medical retirement to civilian life. It was simply part of his make-up now and another reason he took to the open road rather than remain cooped up in a two-up, two-down suburban prison.

'So, do we have any particular schedule, or is this more of an A and E department we're running?' Emily encroached on his half of the room, arms folded across her chest.

'I thought we'd break you in gently today and run more of a walk-in clinic. We can organise something more formal once you're settled, if you prefer.' He operated a casual open-door policy every day but he got the impression this GP would expect something more…structured.

Emily struck him as the type who preferred knowing exactly what she'd be doing from one day to the next without any disruption to her routine. The complete opposite of how he lived his life.

'I'd like to set up a few basic health checks. We could start with taking blood pressure, maybe even a family planning clinic.' She was drifting off into the realms of her own practice but it was a good idea.

Specific clinics might draw in more of the community for preventative check-ups as opposed to waiting until something serious occurred when it was too late to get help from the mainland.

'I think the female population might be more open to you too. Perhaps you could think about running a women's wellness clinic? It's not every day they have someone to talk to them about sensitive subjects such as sexual health or female-specific cancers.' It was as much about educating patients as treating them and he would happily defer to Emily in areas where she had more experience.

'That's a great idea. I'm sure I can put something together for later this week.' Her eyes were shining with excitement rather than fear for the first time since they'd met. Well, if he didn't include last night on her doorstep.

His gaze dropped to her mouth as he relived the memory and the adrenaline rush it had given him. Was giving him. Only her nervous cough snapped him out of his slide back into dangerous territory. He certainly didn't want to freak her out after they'd just established their boundaries.

'Good.'

'Glad we got that sorted.'

It was better all around if they kept their lips to themselves, on different sides of that screen.

There'd been a steady influx of patients throughout the day, more minor ailments than emergency medicine to deal with. Not that she was complaining. Coughs and colds were manageable and it meant she didn't have to call on her colleague for an extra pair of hands. She had, however, handed out a vast amount of paracetamol and antibiotics, not to mention sticking plasters. It was probably a combination of not having these drugs readily available and the novelty of a new, female doctor in residence. At least it showed she'd been accepted in her role and she'd kept busy. That was better than sitting fretting in the corner with nothing but tumbleweeds straying into her section of the clinic. Worse, she'd have had time to overanalyse that kiss some more. Every time he so much as looked in her direction her body went up in flames at the memory. While she was investigating the swollen glands of a pensioner she wasn't thinking about Joe. Much.

'Say "Ah" for me.' She bent over the side of the bed

to peer into her patient's mouth and felt a nudge against her backside.

She turned around to read the Riot Act to whoever it was getting handsy with her when she saw the shadow on the other side of the curtain. Joe was innocently tending his patient too and proving that having little room to manoeuvre was going to be an issue if the butt-bumping became a regular occurrence. It mightn't faze him but she was finding it pretty distracting.

'Your tonsils are quite inflamed but it's nothing a course of antibiotics won't clear up.'

She heard Joe prescribe the same treatment she'd been dishing out all day. It wasn't unusual for viruses to spread like wildfire in such a small community and she was glad of the extra supplies she'd brought with her. They were going to need them, along with the hand sanitiser and vitamin tablets she'd be using to prevent succumbing to it herself. The last thing she needed was Joe having to tend her too.

If the claustrophobic room wasn't hot enough, the thought of her next-door neighbour mopping her fevered brow was enough to bring on the vapours.

Emily moved closer to the oscillating fan before the heat in her cheeks eroded her camouflage make-up and caught sight of a young woman running up the path with a baby in her arms.

'Help! She's not breathing!'

The baby, no more than nine or ten months, was conscious but not making a sound, even though her limbs were flailing in a panic. Not hearing a baby cry in this situation was heart-stopping for her too, indicating the child's airway was completely blocked.

'Give her to me. Quick.'

The child's lips and fingernails were already turning blue but there was no visible sign of obstruction in her mouth.

Joe was at her side in the blink of an eye. 'What happened?'

'She… We were eating breakfast. She grabbed some bread off my plate. Is she going to be okay?'

Emily slid one arm under the baby's back so her hand cradled the head. With her other arm placed on the baby's front, she gently flipped the tiny patient so she was lying face down along her other forearm. She kept the head supported and lower than the bottom and rested her arm against her thigh for added support. With the heel of her hand she hit the baby firmly on the back between the shoulder blades, trying to dislodge whatever was stuck in there.

Delivering a blow to such a small body wasn't easy to do without guilt but the pressure and vibration in the airway was often enough to clear it.

Unfortunately, after the recommended five back blows there was no progress. Time was of the essence as the lack of oxygen to the brain would soon become critical. She rushed over to lay the baby on the bed, paying no mind as Joe kicked the screen away so he had room to assist. He cradled the infant's head, murmuring soothing words for child and mother as Emily started chest thrusts.

With two fingertips she pushed inwards and upwards against the breastbone, trying to shift the blockage. She waited for the chest to return to its normal position before she repeated the action. Her skin was clammy with perspiration as she fought to help the child to breathe. If this didn't work they'd run out of options.

Joe reached out to touch her arm. 'I've done a few tracheostomies in my time if it comes to it.'

He was willing to step up to the plate with her and she found that reassuring. She'd never performed one and hoped it wouldn't come to that. The idea of making an incision for a tube into the windpipe of one so small was terrifying.

'Thank you.'

With her surgical inexperience and the primitive facilities she was glad to have the backup but it was absolutely the last resort. His calm demeanour in the face of a crisis helped her to centre herself again and deliver another chest thrust.

She checked inside the mouth again. If this didn't work she would repeat the cycle before letting Joe take over. After another chest thrust she felt movement beneath her fingers and heard a small cry.

'You've got it!' Joe's shout confirmed her success and she stopped so he could retrieve the chunk of bread causing the trouble.

The colour slowly returned to the baby's face and Emily had never been so relieved to hear a child cry.

'Thank you. Thank you.' The weeping mother alternated between hugging them and stroking her daughter's face.

'I just want to sound her chest.' Emily unhooked her stethoscope from around her neck so she could listen to the baby's heartbeat and make sure there was no resulting damage from the trauma. Her lungs were certainly in good order as she raged her disapproval.

Once she'd carried out her checks and made sure all was well, she gave the relieved mother the go-ahead to comfort her child.

'I think I need to keep you all under observation for a while. Emily, if you don't mind, I'm going to break into that stash of tea and biscuits I saw you put in your locker earlier. We all need it for shock.' Joe's worried frown had evened out into a relieved smile to match her own. She sat down on the bed and waited for the much-needed cup of tea, still feeling a tad shaky herself after the ordeal.

Having a partner here mightn't be all bad. He'd let her take the lead today while still providing support, and tea, when she'd needed it. It made practical sense for them to work together. If only she'd stop overreacting to the slightest body contact. And staring at his backside as he bent down to retrieve her precious cure-all.

CHAPTER FOUR

'I THINK WE deserve a break,' Joe waved off their first emergency patient and her mother at the door once they were sure she had fully recovered.

'I was under the impression we'd just had one.' While it had all been very dramatic and draining, saving lives was part of their job. It shouldn't be an excuse to shut up shop and act unprofessionally. If anything it highlighted the need for them to keep to a schedule so people knew where to reach them at any given time.

'Even busy doctors are entitled to a lunch break. Are you telling me you don't take one back home?' His raised eyebrow and smirk dared her to deny it.

'Of course I take my regulation breaks. Just not usually all at once.' She omitted to mention she took a packed lunch and did her paperwork through those breaks since it made her sound as if she had no life outside work.

He made a derisory '*pfft*' sound through his teeth. 'Ten minutes off our feet, keeping a baby under observation, isn't a real break. We need a proper time out to de-stress before our next patients, otherwise how can we do our jobs effectively? You need to learn how to go with the flow, Emily.'

His cheeky wink only served to irritate her further.

'I thought that's what I *was* doing.' The sigh of self-pity was entirely justified, she thought, after coming all the way out here and taking part in everything thrown at her thus far. If she let herself get carried away too much there was a danger she'd end up completely lost at sea.

'It's lunch, Emily. It's not a big deal.'

It *would* seem silly to him but in her head it translated to something much bigger—ditching their responsibilities for their own gratification. That was exactly what Greg had done and she'd been the one left to deal with the consequences. It wasn't a situation she intended to re-create any time soon.

'What about cover? We can't abandon our post here and leave people without adequate care.'

'We can put a note on the door but, honestly, we won't be that hard to track down if something happens. Yasi Island has survived all this time without us and I'm sure they'll cope over one lunchtime.' He was already scribbling on a piece of paper now he'd made her concerns seem ridiculous.

She was here for two weeks, had treated one emergency patient so far, and was trying to avoid a shared break under the cover of her 'they can't live without me' excuse. It was no wonder he wasn't buying it. This was about him, and her fear of spending time with him, and nothing else. She had to get over it or the next fortnight was going to be hell.

'Is there some place we can buy lunch? I don't recall seeing any fast-food restaurants nearby.' Her tongue-in-cheek comment was intended to make her seem less of a jobsworth but the practicalities of his proposal were no less important to her. While it was refreshing not to have a coffee shop or burger joint on every inch of land, there was also a distinct lack of grocery outlets. She had literally nothing to bring to the table and it wouldn't be polite to help herself to Miriama's meagre provisions.

'Lack of refrigeration is a problem on the island when the only electricity available is via the odd generator here and there so most of the food is fresh. There's none of your fast-frozen, pre-packed, no-taste, processed muck here. The gathering of food is a communal effort, as is eating it. There'll be no shortage of hosts to take lunch with.' He pinned the note to the door and hovered, clearly waiting for her to leave with him.

She was certain the idea of turning up at people's homes uninvited and unannounced was something he did all the time, given his nonchalance now, but she was used to a certain etiquette. Dinner parties and organised soirées were more her thing than breaking bread with strangers. Honestly, this man had no shame.

'Should we take a gift?' Something to break the ice and make it seem less like begging for food. She'd rather starve than face any humiliation.

'You've already donated supplies to the school and I thought we could head there first. The children will be thrilled to meet you. They enjoy showing off and I know for a fact this is their lunchtime too. So...' He gestured for her to make her way out in front of him but she wasn't entirely convinced by his argument. That 'first' comment alluded to the idea there'd be more than one stop.

'You could take your medical bag with you if that makes you any more comfortable about leaving.' He pre-empted her next attempt to back out.

'A mobile clinic?' It wasn't a bad idea to combine work and lunch, and accepting their hospitality in exchange for her medical skills was much more palatable than simply pulling up a chair and waiting to be served.

'If that's what you'd prefer.' His voice was a mixture of amusement and exasperation.

'It is.' She knew she could be hard work when people seemed to tire of her so easily but at least Joe nudged her with encouragement rather than criticism. It left her free to make decisions on her own terms.

Negotiations over, she grabbed her bag and followed him out the door. Despite her initial reservations, reaching this compromise felt like a win. With a little forward planning she could *do* spontaneity. Somewhere between Joe's laid-back attitude and her regimented approach to work they might find a way to actually make this work. Perhaps if she found that happy medium in her personal life, she might make that work again too.

Joe had been right again. It was becoming a habit. And very annoying. Every time his cool, calm and rational thinking was proved correct it made her fears seem all the more neurotic.

Their impromptu visit to the school had caused such a commotion the children had immediately abandoned their lessons. She would've felt terribly guilty about the disruption if their teacher hadn't been equally animated by their arrival.

'*Vanaku.* Thank you for coming to see the children.'

The pupils all stood to attention behind their desks as though someone of great importance had entered the room. It was difficult to come to terms with the fact that person could be her.

'I, er…we thought I should come and introduce myself. I'm Emily, the new doctor.' She shook hands with the pretty young teacher.

'I'm Keresi. We're so grateful for your wonderful gifts to the school. Aren't we, children?'

They were prompted into an enthusiastic chorus of agreement that managed to suffuse Emily's cheeks with heat.

'It's nothing, really.' She'd only brought a few stationery supplies at the last minute. Nothing that would've warranted such an outpouring of gratitude at home. It was humbling to be reminded how lucky she was in the grand scheme of things and how much she took for granted. Okay, her heart had taken a mauling recently but she'd had a university education that enabled her to live a life of luxury compared to many here.

'We would really like to do something for you.' The effusive teacher clapped her hands to assemble the kids along the back wall of the classroom.

Emily stepped further into the room to allow Joe in on whatever was about to happen. No matter how hard she tried to make this a solo adventure they were destined to share these experiences and if she was honest, everything seemed slightly less intimidating when he was close by. This morning had been a prime example. She'd coped with the emergency largely on her own but having him there had been a comfort when she was so far from the medical support she was used to. Joe had been the first person in a long time to make sure she hadn't felt alone.

The children launched into a repertoire of songs and dance, so well choreographed she understood this must be something they performed on a regular basis for tourists—and hungry doctors. It enabled her to stop over-analysing what people would think of her for turning up uninvited and enjoy the proud display of talent. Old and young alike had made it impossible not to be a part of the community here.

Once the show was over, she and Joe broke into applause.

'That was just…lovely.' The tears in her eyes and lump in her throat arrived unexpectedly.

'Yes, thanks, everybody.' Joe lifted his hands above his head and gave them another round of applause.

'We're going to take our lunch outside now, if you'd

care to join us.' Keresi motioned her class outside as she delivered the invitation Joe had prophesied.

'That's so kind of you. We'd be honoured. Wouldn't we, Emily?' He didn't even attempt to hide his glee at being proved right.

'Sure, and in return we'd be happy to do a free health check for everyone while we're here.'

She'd call that an even trade and a conscience salve all in one.

With everyone in accordance and no one beholden to anyone else, the trio of adults joined the rest of the class outside on the grass.

Joe had made it sound as though lunch would be some grand affair with buffet-style tables of food, or at least that's how she'd interpreted it. Instead, the children were cross-legged under the shade of the trees, tucking into their food boxes.

'What are we going to do? A lunch-box raid?' she murmured, before catching herself.

She cleared her throat to draw his attention and spoke again. 'I'm not taking food from the mouths of babes.'

'Will you chill out? I can guarantee you'll neither have to ask for food while you're here nor starve. Honestly, you put yourself through so much unnecessary stress you'll make yourself ill. You should take a leaf out of your brother's book and take this all in your stride.' He rested his large hand on her shoulder in an act that should've been easy for her to shrug off along with his advice, but his warmth on her bare skin stole away any snarky retort. His touch had distracted her even from the arrival of her stepbrother, who was strolling towards them.

'Hey, you two. I saw your note and figured you might want to share a bite to eat.' He held up a basket of fresh fruit and other foods not readily identifiable to Emily. At this moment she didn't care. Her stomach was rumbling and Peter was family. She was entitled to take food from him guilt-free.

'Oh, ye of little faith.'

Joe was really going to keep this gloating going all day.

Thankfully he did release her from his thrall, abandoning her shoulder in favour of a banana. There was definitely a happy vibe about him, her brother too, which was surprising given their previous life before Yasi. It showed a definite strength of character in both of them to have come through the darkness that time in Afghanistan had surely brought to their door.

She kind of envied this enlightened attitude they'd found where they no longer sweated the small stuff and trusted that everything would somehow work out in the end. Although not the path, or the losses they'd endured to reach this Zen place. A place that seemed so far beyond her reach when even the timely food delivery was causing concern.

'Er...what is this?' She prodded the leafy parcels that were apparently the main component of their meal.

'*Rourou* and cassava,' Peter declared, as though that helped her identify what he expected her to eat. Time apart had made him forget who he was dealing with here. This was the girl who'd taken a great deal of persuading to partake of the mildest curries when they'd gone to an Indian restaurant for the first time. She needed any new dish explained in simple layman's terms and a tasting demonstration before she ventured into new territory.

Joe had no such qualms as he dug in with his fingers to take a sample. 'They're *dalo* leaves with boiled tapioca.'

'Just like real school dinners, then?' With her food taster apparently unharmed, and Peter helping himself too, Emily braved the unknown. It wasn't as bad tasting as she'd imagined and the starchy snack would fuel her for the rest of the afternoon, along with the more familiar fruit she took for later.

'I know you'd rather have a pasta salad and a fruit smoothie but this is the next best thing. You'll get used to it. I have.' Peter took a second helping to prove his point.

'I see that.' She also saw the way his gaze kept drifting past her to watch the pretty Keresi in the background.

'Did you make these, bro?' Joe scooped up the last food bundle after she declined it.

Her taste buds had been enjoying the sweet and stodgy delights of comfort food these past months so it was going to take some time to adjust.

'No. The young mother whose baby you saved this morning sent them over to say thank-you. You two are her new heroes.'

'Hey, it was all your sister. This girl knows her stuff and I wouldn't want to get on the wrong side of her by claiming credit for what she did. She can hit pretty hard when she wants to.' Joe held his hands up and deflected the praise back to her.

'Oh, I know all about it. She can be vicious if you take her toys without permission and as for her chocolate stash, if you touch that your life won't be worth living.' Peter made it sound as though they'd had a tempestuous relationship growing up when nothing could be further from the truth. She'd been so happy to be accepted by him and his mum, Shirl, she'd followed him like a puppy. He'd have been justified in pushing his pesky shadow away but he'd never once made her feel like a nuisance or his ugly stepsister. She'd often thought how different her life could've been if Shirl had been her *actual* mother, avoiding all the unpleasantness of her early years.

Peter rubbed the invisible evidence of their imaginary argument on his leg but his eyes were still focused on something, someone else. That someone who was making her way over to their little group.

'Can I get you a drink?'

'That would be—'

'I'll help you.' Peter cut her off as he stumbled to his feet in a hurry.

'Could he be any more obvious?' Emily's eye-roll was born out of her irrational jealousy that there was now a third party competing for his attention. She may as well have been back in high school when he had been the popular kid and she'd been the newbie with no friends of her own.

'Give him a break.'

'I thought he was here to spread the word of God, not get romantically involved with his congregation.' She'd never seen him so smitten as he trailed after his love interest into the school, his tongue practically hanging out, but she shouldn't be a brat and put her own happiness above Peter's. This lovestruck bohemian was a far cry from the traumatised veteran she'd last encountered and his healing was all that mattered.

'He's a red-blooded, single man, not a monk, and this place is doing him the world of good. He'll be settled down with two point four kids before you know it.' Joe plucked a blade of grass from the ground and wound it around his finger until the circulation stopped and it turned white.

Despite his wise words on the subject he didn't look any more thrilled about that prospect than she did. He was supposed to be the fly-by-the-seat-of-his-pants adventurer, not a stick-in-the-mud who hated change like her.

'And you? Are you planning on settling down at some point?' Her heart fluttered as she asked the question, which had been on her mind since he'd kissed her.

His snort-laugh cut any hope dead that she could be

the one to make him think again about his nomadic life choice but it was better to face that truth now before she got carried away over the next few days and considered that a possibility.

'No chance. These itchy feet of mine don't let me hang around long enough to develop that kind of attachment.'

'Why's that?' It would've made more sense to her that someone who'd been in a war zone would've been glad of the normality and stability that a family could bring.

He was pulling the grass out in clumps now. 'Life's too short not to get out there and experience everything the world has to offer. I'm never going to be the pipe-and-slippers type to sit and vegetate in front of the telly with his missus.'

There was the crux of Emily's ill-judged attraction towards him. If you swapped the pipe for a bar of chocolate he'd just described her idea of a perfect night in.

He hadn't mentioned the events leading to his retirement from the army but she guessed that was part of the reason for his compulsion to live life to the full. In that sense he and her brother were very alike. The blast had had a profound impact on how they lived from day to day and she was in awe of their courage when any new experience brought her out in a cold sweat. If, on the other hand, this drifting from one place to the next had been the guys running away from dealing with what had happened, setting down roots was a huge step forward. Still, long-term relationships didn't always equal a happy-ever-after.

'Yeah, marriage sucks,' she said, trying to convince herself she didn't want or need it any more either.

Joe raised his eyebrows at her as he stood and brushed the grass from his hands. Now she was going to have to explain herself and confess she was one of those losers who'd tried and failed at it.

'I'm divorced. Greg left me for another woman.' Even

in the shade she was burning with the shame of her husband's rejection. Although it was almost a relief to say it out loud.

Colleagues and friends knew about the split but she hadn't divulged the gory details. Blurting it out to a man she'd only met and most likely would never see again was liberating. She could vent without fear of repercussions.

He held out his hand to help her up and without missing a beat said, 'He's an idiot.'

Those three simple words brought a smile to her lips and a lightness in her heart. There was no changing of the subject or querying the circumstances, he'd simply decided in her favour. Greg *was* an idiot and she should stop wasting any more of her life on him.

Joe's lifestyle sounded too lonely for her but she could appreciate its merits. There was an attraction in walking away from a relationship before things got too serious and certain expectations grew around it. Such as being together for ever. Avoiding love was the best way to protect your heart. Thank goodness she no longer trusted anyone with hers.

CHAPTER FIVE

JOE'S PLAN TO get outside of their confined workspace into the great outdoors to create some distance between him and Emily had backfired spectacularly. Somehow mingling with a large group of excited school children had led to lunch together discussing their private lives, or in his case a lack of one. Where Emily's was concerned he'd call it a lucky escape.

Peter didn't usually take against people without due cause but when he talked about his ex-brother-in-law it had never been with any degree of affection. It would take a certain kind of someone to get him offside when he was such a people person. The sort who imagined he could do better than Emily. *Idiot* wasn't a strong enough word to describe what Joe thought of the guy but it was the only tag he could give him in the presence of children.

Although it was early days to be thinking of Peter and the schoolteacher as being in a serious relationship, leading to something more permanent, it certainly seemed to be heading that way. It caused him mixed emotions. He was happy to see his friend in such a great place after struggling with his faith in the aftermath of Afghanistan and it meant he himself was no longer obligated to stick around as his sole support system. Peter settled down would give him the freedom to move on to his next adventure free from residual responsibility that kept him tied to his old army pal. It certainly shouldn't create the extra hole in his heart and a pang for the life he'd never have.

He couldn't afford to have a wife and children relying on him when he couldn't even depend on himself, on his own emotions. He'd heard somewhere that grief was the price you paid for loving someone but he really didn't want to go through it again. He'd loved Batesy and Ste like brothers, grieved for them as part of his army family, and shouldered responsibility for their loss as any other medic who'd lost patients would have. It was impossible not to become that close to anyone and not feel compassion again. He was risking his heart and his sanity by remaining in the medical field but it was still his calling. These pop-up clinics were a compromise, his answer to preventing further long-term damage to his soul while still being able to treat those in desperate need. Listening to Emily's tale of marriage woe was enough to strengthen his resolve on the matter. Commitment to anything beyond a casual arrangement did more harm than good.

Hence this afternoon's impromptu alfresco lunch. Working side by side in that hut had not only led to inadvertent body contact but a growing admiration for his co-worker. This morning had shone a light on her professionalism in what had been a highly emotive and dramatic case, the like of which she probably wasn't used to in her day job. He shouldn't be surprised, she was a qualified doctor after all, but he'd clearly been thinking about her in a less than professional manner.

Romantic picnics in the park weren't going to help get his mind back in the game but the clinic idea at the school had helped re-establish the boundaries of their relationship. For the past couple of hours they'd been busy chatting to the children and making sure they were all in tip-top health, with Emily on one side of the room and him on the other. Except now her queue of children had come to an end and she was making her way over to his table.

'Well, Dr Braden, anything to report?' She was totally at ease here. He could see it in her relaxed body language and the big smile on her lips.

He should really quit paying attention to what her lips were doing at any given moment. It wouldn't help him forget how they felt against his: soft, pliant, agreeable...

There was no way he trusted himself not to try and experience it again if they were holed up in that close space for another two weeks.

'Just another A-star pupil.' He gave his last patient a high five and watched him run off with his last excuse to hang around.

'They're a pretty happy, healthy bunch all round.'

'And more than willing to have a bit of fuss from the glamorous new doctor.' He hadn't missed the girls' fascination with her blonde hair, or the fact she'd let them braid it while she'd worked. The boys too had been more interested in what was going on at that side of the room, which had made their eye checks challenging.

Emily's laughter reached right in and twisted his insides. It was the first time he'd heard it since her arrival and he knew he wanted to hear more of it.

'*Glamorous* isn't the word I'd use right now.' She was finger-brushing the various plaits and knots her army of hairdressers had created, leaving her tresses wavy and unkempt and looking a lot like bed hair.

It conjured up images of her in the morning, in bed, and brought a lot more adjectives to describe her that weren't appropriate in a classroom. Joe had to turn away and pack away the ophthalmoscope and otoscope he'd been using to check the children's eyes and ears before he said or did something stupid. Again.

'Thank you for doing this.' Keresi interrupted Joe's wayward thoughts to shake hands with him and Emily.

'Thanks for letting us disrupt your lessons today. We're going to take our travelling sideshow further afield but I'm sure you could get Peter to track us down in an emergency.' He'd disappeared during their clinic but Joe had a hunch he'd return before the end of the school day.

'Since when?' Emily's mouth flattened out into an unimpressed line once they were alone again. Her mouth was puckered now, her turquoise eyes blazing with flecks of amber fire and her arms folded across her chest as she made her disapproval known. He supposed it would be totally out of order to comment on how hot she looked.

'We've had such a great response here I thought we could venture further around the village with our mobile clinic. A meet and greet with those who might be too busy to attend isn't a bad idea.' In the army he'd learned to think on his feet, and forced with their imminent return to the claustrophobic hub of medical operations he'd made an executive decision. Not to.

'You really need to stop making decisions for other people. You're not in the army now and you're certainly not my superior,' Emily huffed, as she made the scarily accurate call about his thought process. He was railroading her into taking a trail away from his temporary lodgings when they were supposed to be equal partners but separating her from his bed space would be beneficial to them both in the long run.

'Sorry, I'm not used to working with a partner. I should have asked if you would prefer to spend the afternoon bumping into each other and waiting for people to show up or go out and drum up some interest in your clinic.' He didn't think of it as emotional blackmail, more as forward planning. Once Emily had her own patients set up they could alternate between running both static and mobile practices. With some organisation he could engineer the rest of her stay so they spent minimal time in each other's company.

'When you put it like that I guess it's a no-brainer.' She stuck her tongue out at him in a manner more like that of a friend than a professional colleague. Definitely time to make that distinction between them. There wasn't room in his life even for a friend. He already had one more than he needed. It was the only reason he'd stayed on Yasi as long as he had. He would never have stood back and ignored Peter's pleas for help out here when he still felt as though he had a huge debt to repay. As soon as his stint here was over and all necessary referrals to the hospital on the mainland had been made, he was gone. Ready to disappear into anonymity again and start over somewhere where they didn't know his history.

Their stroll through the village in the daylight was taken at a more leisurely pace than last night's constitutional. Out here in public view with the sights and sounds of island life around them somehow felt less intense, safer. Even if it hadn't taken away the urge to kiss her.

'What's that growing on the roof up there?' Emily pointed at the rows of brown string covering which, to the untrained eye, could've been mistaken for decaying foliage.

'That's coconut husk. They dry the strands in the sun before they braid it. *Magimagi* is the main source of income here. Children are taught the skill from a very early age. Unfortunately, even with all the hard work that goes into it, it sells for a pittance. You're talking only a few dollars for about twenty-five yards of handmade rope.'

'Wow. I don't know whether to admire the work ethos or pity the folks who do it. I'll never complain about my long hours again. At least I get paid a living wage.'

'Both. It's part and parcel of living here. Unless you're a blow-in, of course, who's benefiting from the local hospitality.'

'Don't make me feel any guiltier about accepting food and lodging than I already do.'

Her genuine outrage made him chuckle. Emily would no more take advantage of people than her generous-spirited stepbrother. From what he'd gathered about her personal life, he suspected it was probably the other way around. It would be so easily for a manipulative sort to tie her soft heart into knots to suit their own agenda. She'd had enough of that in her life for him to do the same. His actions were merely to protect her as well as himself.

'I'm only joking. Everything given to you here is simply payment for all the work you're doing to help the community. Think of that as your wages, then there's no need to feel guilty.' At least, that's how he viewed it when the doubts crept in about accepting so much from those who had so little. It wasn't as though rejecting their gifts of friendship was an option when it would cause even greater offence.

'I'll try to remember that,' she said, a tad more brightly, clearly never having considered the work she was doing here as anything more than the job she was born to do. That humility made her all the more special.

She had that same warrior spirit of every man he'd ever fought alongside—selflessly giving of herself without expecting anything in return. Unfortunately she didn't recognise her own strengths, only her weaknesses. The sooner she found them herself, the sooner he'd be off the hook.

'You should. You'll definitely earn your keep over the next two weeks. The community as a whole will make the most of having qualified medical personnel, even if there are a few too busy trying to make a living to visit.'

'The *magimagi* weavers?'

'And the rest of the arts and crafts community. The economy here is based on the sale of handmade goods such as wooden sculptures and woven mats. If you're lucky you might get to try making some for yourself.' He was counting on it. Okay, so his service to the community wasn't as selfless as Emily's. He'd been part of the scenery here long enough to know that taking her out to that part of the island would be another excuse for a social gathering.

Not only was he spreading the word about the clinic by introducing her but it would certainly help them pass the afternoon. In company.

Emily knew exactly what Joe was up to. He was trying to get her out of his way, palm her off onto someone else. It was the only plausible explanation as to why he was so reluctant they return to what was supposed to be their base of operations. She didn't totally buy this notion of extending personal invitations to her practice when news seemed to travel so quickly across the island anyway.

The kava ceremony was supposed to have been her introduction to society and unless he was using this to ensure he had a dinner invitation too, it felt like a futile exercise. She was only going along with it so she could get a bearing on her surroundings and those she'd be potentially treating. Once she'd established her own list of patients and could manage a conversation without an introduction from her self-appointed leader, she could stop relying on him to get her through this. She wasn't swapping one man-sized crutch for another. This was no journey of self-discovery if Joe was always there showing her the way.

He was a man who craved excitement, thrived on it. The more he did for her, smoothed the way for her, the less interesting she would become to him. As they spent more time together the last thing she wanted was for him to find her just as boring as her husband had.

She'd come here with the idea of reinventing herself as a fearless trailblazer, an inspiration to life's other rejects too afraid to step back out into the sun, only to find herself falling into step behind Joe and following that safe path.

With the warmth of the islanders she was beginning to shed her nerves. There'd been nothing but support for her so far and this morning's drama, although traumatic, had proved her professional worth. The children had been wonderful too, and although another random house call could be seen as skiving she was kind of looking forward to it.

Ten-minute appointments with patients passing through her office on a conveyor belt was frustrating to say the least. At least here she wasn't restrained by time limits or budget; she was free to diagnose and treat anyone who needed her help.

The way of life here was so fascinating and such a far cry from the frantic digital age where she spent more time on the phone or answering emails than getting to know the people she was treating. Time out here had a different meaning, more significance, and gave her extra opportunities to be the best doctor she could be.

'They do say hobbies are a great way to relieve stress. Perhaps I'll find a new creative outlet for my frustrations and irritations.' She batted her eyelashes and smiled a saccharine-sweet smile, enjoying Joe's obvious bewilderment at her sudden compliance.

When it came to interpreting her thoughts and feelings regarding her chaperon she was just as confused. Apart from her own neuroses, he was the main stumbling block between her and her new super-identity. But she'd be lying if she said she didn't appreciate having him as a safety net at times, knowing she could rely on him if she needed support. Plus he was great eye candy. She might have put her heart under lock and key but that didn't mean she was made of stone. She could still appreciate the sight of a perfect male specimen. Especially one flashing his rippling torso as he lifted the hem of his shirt to wipe his brow.

Shallow. So very shallow. She of all people should've resisted objectifying another human being but that flat, toned body deserved recognition. Hell, it deserved its own social media account. She fanned herself with her hand. The heat was starting to get to her and it wasn't entirely down to the fires lining their path through the encampment.

When she managed to drag her gaze away from his midsection and back up to meet his eyes she could see he was more amused than appalled by her visual appreciation.

Busted.

'So, what do they do here?' She coughed away the stirrings his naked chest had caused with a question about the other sights of interest. Okay, steaming pans and bubbling pots weren't nearly as interesting as cheese-grater abs but were infinitely less likely to get her burned.

'This is where they boil the *pandanus* leaves to make them soft enough to weave. They fade from green to white once they're left to dry in the sun before the cloth they make is painted to make colourful mats. It's quite an art.' Joe gave her a quick run-down of the process, displaying more local knowledge than a mere tourist should be privy to.

He might claim to have no attachment to Yasi other than another pin tack on his wall map but it had already become a part of him. Emily wondered if its mystical healing powers would work on her too. Her brother had certainly found his peace on the island and Joe was way too involved in the way of life for someone who'd probably been strong-armed into volunteering here in the first place. If all her wishes came true too this magical isle would conjure up her own successful, independent practice and someone other than her stepbrother who loved her and accepted her for who she was.

The second of those was never going to happen since there was no way in hell she'd forgo her camouflage and let anyone see the *real* her. The best she could hope for was a holiday tan and a good time. After the last year she was willing to settle for that.

He introduced her to Sou and a few of her friends, sitting cross-legged on the floor painting the mats. They welcomed her and immediately invited her to stop clutching her medical bag as though she'd come to sell them encyclopaedias and join them.

Furniture was overrated anyway. Along with the internet and hot running water. And abs. A girl could live without all of them. If she had to.

She didn't want to interrupt their working day but they were keen to start a new mat in her honour and have her be a part of it.

'What kind of paint is this?' she asked as the ladies coloured black geometric shapes with earthy red tones.

'The black is made from ash and coal from the fire mixed with water. It can be messy.' Sou gave her a toothy smile as she prepared the primitive materials in a bowl with her hands.

'The red is actually from clay found on the island. It's scraped and rinsed with water to create various shades.' Although this activity appeared to be primarily women's work, Joe happily took up a place beside her on the floor.

'You've done this before?' Was there anything left for her to explore on the island that he hadn't already laid claim to? She wanted to be annoyed at the unintentional one-upmanship but it was impossible when he didn't have a bad bone in his body. And she'd thoroughly inspected it.

He didn't seem to care about losing face at sitting in the midst of all the women, when his joy at sharing his newly acquired skill with her was plain to see.

This mat-painting session was Yasi's equivalent to a coffee morning, as Emily soon found out. The ladies spent their time swapping anecdotes and chatting among themselves but she was finding it tough to pay attention to everything going on around her when her gaze was locked onto that of the smiling hunk next to her.

'You dip your finger in the clay mixture.' He took her hand in his and pressed her fingertip firmly into the red sludge. 'Then it's simply a matter of colouring between the lines.' He leaned across to guide her between the thick black outlines.

His breath was hot against her neck and her own was caught somewhere between a squeak and a squeal as it brought goose-bumps along her skin. Somehow she managed to daub enough paint on to fill the small triangle she'd been assigned. Amazing when his touch had turned her into a ragdoll with no control over her floppy limbs except by his hand.

Only when he excused himself from the group to go and visit the wood-carving menfolk outside was she able to breathe and move freely again. She could inhale a lungful of fresh air no longer contaminated by his spicy, exotic scent, which had made every breath feel as though she was taking part of him inside her.

'That man is handsome!' Sou's unlikely outburst was accompanied by the giggles of grown women with a girlish crush.

Emily gave a nervous laugh along with them, grateful she wasn't the only one finding his charms irresistible.

'And single!' There was another titter of female appreciation. Clearly, getting het up around this man was a normal reaction and nothing for Emily to worry about.

'Are you two together?'

It took a moment before Emily recognised they'd stopped gossiping among themselves and were addressing her directly. Four pairs of eyes were watching her unblinkingly and waiting for her answer.

'No. No.' She couldn't keep the hint of regret from her voice when she was still recovering from her up close and personal painting tutorial.

'Why not?' Sou tilted her head to one side and stared at her as though she was trying to work out what was wrong with her.

'We're colleagues and I only arrived twenty-four hours ago.' Emily dodged eye contact and concentrated on staying between the lines so no one would see the naked desire for him she was fighting with every breath.

As she stared at her discoloured fingertips and shuffled position so her legs didn't fall asleep, it struck her how off track her itinerary for this trip had gone. Other than the ladies promising to drop in at the clinic, this had nothing to do with her duties as a doctor.

Sou made a strange grunting noise, which sounded like something between disbelief and bewilderment. 'I can tell he likes you.'

The others nodded and clucked their agreement like hens around her.

'Really?' As much as Emily was uncomfortable about her and Joe being the topic of conversation, their reassurance created a warm glow inside her. She wanted him to like her, to see her as more than his mate's kid sister he was obliged to take under his wing, and to think of her as more than a colleague. The way she was doing about him.

There was more clucking.

'I can see it in the way he looks at you. The way he touches you.'

'Oh, yes!'

'Mmm-hmm.'

Another chorus of oohs and laughter sent Emily's temperature rising with the heat of being in the spotlight. Perhaps it hadn't simply been a case of wishful thinking after all.

She cast her mind back over their interaction with a different eye. Had there really been a need to hold her hand? Or sit that close? There was also the matter of that kiss. Dared she hope there'd been more to it than she'd convinced herself? And what if there was? Did she want to go there and start kissing a man she barely knew and wouldn't see again?

Every time she envisaged going through the same heartache Greg had caused her, she pictured Joe instead with his smile and gentle consideration. The answer was overwhelmingly yes, she wanted to kiss him again.

It was the possibility of rejection that frightened her, that abandonment she'd suffered too often, but at the end of this trip *she* would be the one walking away. The whole idea was that she went back to England a stronger person, a braver one for the risks she *should* take. It was time to woman up and live dangerously, and there was nothing more terrifying than the prospect of dipping a toe back into the dating pool. What better way to reintroduce herself than with a holiday romance?

She smiled to herself.

The room erupted into laughter around her.

'Just co-workers, huh?'

'Emily, you've got it bad.'

Yes, yes, she had and it was within her power to turn it into something good.

CHAPTER SIX

JOE SWUNG THE axe and brought it crashing down to split the timber in two. It was a powerful blow designed to be effective both physically and mentally. He'd needed to be in the company of men, doing manly things. Not more hand-holding and making memories with his pretty co-worker. It was all very well making sure they were in a public place but it kind of defeated the object of avoiding close contact if he couldn't leave her side.

He'd been carried away with the whole tour-guide demonstration with the *masi* process because she'd been so open to it. A complete attitude turnaround since the kava ceremony and he hadn't been able to resist capitalising on her new willingness to participate in the local culture. It wasn't often he got to share new experiences with anyone and showing her how to paint the mats had given him the same buzz as when he'd tried it for the first time.

So engrossed in that moment of her new discovery, he'd forgotten the reasons they were there in the first place. Patients. Work. Education. Definitely not taking part in couples' activities as if they were at a holiday camp together. He'd remembered that too late—after the touching and the quickening pulse as he'd leaned too close to the flame.

He'd made a bolt for it in an attempt to direct the adrenaline coursing through his body toward something more practical than neck-kissing his colleague in public. The sculptors had given him the job of sanding the wooden bowls they sold for mixing kava but the smooth, silky texture hadn't really detracted his thoughts away from Emily's skin beneath his touch. So he'd moved on to the more demanding task of preparing the raw material for them in the hope he'd be too exhausted to keep thinking about her. It clearly hadn't worked.

His time hadn't totally been wasted as he'd persuaded a few of the men to stop by the clinic before the end of the week for blood-pressure checks and a general 'MOT'. If Emily had stuck to the plan she'd have a few more re-cruits on her side too.

'I think we have enough now, Joe, and the light's start-ing to fade.' Tomasi, Sou's other half, was the one to fi-nally call time.

Joe had been concentrating so hard on making sure he chopped the wood in half and not his foot, he hadn't no-ticed the sun beginning to set. In the name of health and safety he would have to call it a day. Besides, they had enough wood stacked now to last for weeks.

'I guess I was enjoying my workout too much.' He snatched up his shirt from the top of the wood pile where he'd thrown it after working up a sweat.

'Sou says we're welcome to stay for dinner...'

Joe glanced up as Emily's voice trailed off at the door-way to find her staring again, her mouth open but no fur-ther words forthcoming. Her eyes travelled up and down his body without ever reaching his. There was no other word for it. She was *ogling* him.

He made a bigger deal of unfolding his shirt and pull-ing it over his head than he really needed to, giving her more time to look. No woman had stared at him with such naked desire since the explosion, or if they had he hadn't noticed or found it quite so enjoyable.

He'd flirted and slept with women since leaving the army but a part of his male pride had died along with all his other losses. Although it was only his hearing that had been damaged in the blast he'd stopped thinking of himself as a 'whole' man. With Emily watching him dress as though he could've been the world's sexiest male model instead of a disabled ex-soldier, he made the most of every second of it. She was a doctor who'd probably seen better bodies than his over the space of her career but her apparent fascination was proof this attraction wasn't one-sided. Not that he knew what he should do about that, if anything, when it would only complicate everything.

'Sou has…er…invited us inside for a bite to eat.' Emily slowly came out of her trance now that those hypnotic abs of steel had been hidden from view. Thanks to the T-shirt's shield of invisibility, his hold on her was temporarily suspended. She pretended she was squinting into the semi-darkness, trying to see him, rather than getting her rocks off staring at him half-naked.

'Is that what you want to do?'

Damn him, he'd deployed that adorable smile to disguise his dirty tactics. He was forcing her to make the decision.

'It would be rude not to.' She'd spent the past couple of hours in their company, being part of their group, as Joe had done with the men. It wouldn't be right to shun their invitation now, especially when she had nothing to rush back to. Unlike her *real* life, she wasn't planning her evening to catch up on paperwork or binge-watch episodes of her favourite TV shows.

Dinner with friendly islanders and a hunky ex-serviceman could be the most exotic meal she'd ever have in her life.

Take that, boring old Emily Clifford!

It turned out to be every bit as extraordinary as she'd imagined. The men and women all gathered inside Sou and Tomasi's house and took up their places on the floor mats. The women had put together a feast while Emily had finished up her painting and Joe had been flexing his muscles outside. Although she remained wary about the contents of the dishes laid before her, she had Joe on hand to sample the menu for her first.

With no cutlery available she had no choice but to follow suit and eat with her hands. She chose a pork dish and something delicious called *palusami*, which Joe explained was spinach prepared in coconut cream, and washed it down with a cup of black tea. With her belly full she realised she was getting the hang of this immersion into Yasi society. The only times her nerves had bunched together to remind her this wasn't the norm for her had been when Joe had brushed against her and made her tingle with sexual awareness.

It was a blessing the others hadn't continued with their teasing because she was pretty sure she was doing a bang-up job of making a fool of herself without their help. She'd been positively drooling as she'd watched his topless axe work and tensed every time he leaned in to explain the menu to her, like some virgin schoolgirl with a crush on her teacher. Her emotions had been stretched to every conceivable extreme today and although she was glad to end it in such good company, the walk home was playing on her mind. Their last one had ended in *that* kiss and she was so tightly wound after this evening she might explode if she didn't get the release she'd been craving since his lips had first touched hers.

'Don't forget to take your *masi* with you.' Sou presented her with the finished mat, which already held so many memories for her, when she stood to leave.

'Thank you. That's so kind of you.' They'd spent hours working on it. Time that should have been channelled into their livelihood. It was a wonderful gesture that choked her up even though she should expect this level of kindness by now.

'A souvenir of your time here.'

Emily didn't miss Sou's gaze flicker between her and Joe, a silent insistence she attributed significance to *all* of tonight's events.

'I'll cherish the memories of everyone here,' she assured her with a wry smile. Tonight wouldn't easily be forgotten, with or without the satisfactory conclusion of a second, perhaps more passionate lip-lock.

Emily retrieved her long-forgotten medical bag from the corner of the room. If today had taught her anything apart from her apparent weakness for muscular medics, it was that an office and an appointment book was no substitute for getting out and experiencing life. It was no wonder Greg had grown tired of her if this was what he'd been doing while she'd remained stagnant.

After all the sweetness she'd tasted today, the thought that her inability to spread her wings beyond her own living room had killed her marriage left a sour taste in her mouth. The only consolation she had was that wherever Greg was, whatever he was doing, it couldn't compare with her current adventure.

'Is everything all right, Emily? I know you didn't particularly want to leave the clinic but, honestly, we'd have heard about any emergency.' Joe's concern as they waved their goodbyes reinforced the idea she spoiled everyone's fun by always playing by the rules.

She'd gambled a few times over this last couple of

days and the world hadn't stopped turning because she'd
swapped her sensible shoes for some frivolous flip-flops.
Far from creating a catastrophic shift in the universe,
these spontaneous acts had added a new, fun dimension
to her existence.

Each new accepted challenge had enriched her time
here with new friends, new skills and tastes, and the new
memories were starting to dim the unpleasant ones she'd
accumulated recently. One of which topped them all.
Every time Greg's cruel words came back to haunt her
she'd replace the image of his mouth curled in a sneer as
he turned her heart inside out with one of Joe. His lips
soft and tender on hers and leaving her fuzzy inside instead of cold.

She sighed. 'It's not that. I just couldn't help thinking that perhaps if I'd been a different woman then, this
woman, perhaps Greg wouldn't have left me for someone else.'

Joe frowned at her with a scorn she hadn't expected
after their evening playing nice. 'Is that what you want? To
waste your life on someone who doesn't appreciate you for
who you are? Did you ever think that *he* should've been
a different man, a better husband, someone you weren't
afraid to try new things with?'

Someone like Joe.

She'd never considered that take on the situation and
had simply accepted the blame for the breakdown in their
relationship as she had when her mother had left. Neither
had wanted to be with her any more and since she had
been the common denominator it was logical to assume
she had been the root cause. They had wanted her to be
someone else to suit their needs but she hadn't found that
out until it was too late.

The truth was she couldn't pinpoint one specific reason why Greg had cheated on her and effectively ended

their marriage. Yes, he'd said she was boring but she'd been the same woman he'd married. She hadn't changed, he had. One morning he'd simply woken up and decided he could do better. He'd simply grown tired of her and decided he no longer wanted her in his life. That thought had kept her awake and tearful for a long time. It didn't do a lot for a girl who was faced with her own faults in the mirror every single morning. She didn't want to hold on to that negativity any more.

'No.' To all of it. Including Greg.

'Good.' Joe took the mat and helped share her load.

She'd been clinging to the idea of marriage, not the realities of it. Working long days and being expected to have dinner waiting for her husband the minute he walked through the door had been a juggling act. In order to be the perfect wife she hadn't even confronted him on those times he'd arrived home late without an explanation, food ruined and a complete waste of her time cooking it. After the shock of his infidelity those overrunning meetings and last-minute business trips had taken on a sinister new meaning. She'd taken his word his absences were work-related, too trusting to even contemplate it was all lies to cover his dalliances with another woman. Or women. Her trust had been shattered to the point she'd no longer known who it was she'd married.

She'd never forgive him for what he'd put her through, regardless of how much he'd insisted it was her fault he'd chased excitement elsewhere. A marriage was supposed to be a partnership based on love, trust and communication. None of which it turned out they'd had. He hadn't even given her the chance to fix anything when he'd ditched her rather than discuss their problems like a normal couple. Although it hadn't seemed like it up until now, being on her own was probably better than going through the motions of a sham marriage. It had only taken some good company and straight talking for her to finally see that.

She didn't want to waste another second on regrets. That included not acting on the sexual chemistry between her and Joe. Not that she was intending to seduce him or anything, that would be a step too far, but even initiating another kiss seemed such a thrilling prospect it was all she could think about. The spectre of rejection always haunted her actions but he'd kissed her first, looked at her the way she'd lusted after him and lessened the chances he'd spurn her. It was the next big step in becoming Emily Jackson again.

Except she'd spent so long overthinking how she should approach this they were almost back at her door. So much for being spontaneous. She'd never learned how to flirt, had never had reason to. The ugly duckling would've been laughed out of high school if she'd even attempted it and it had been Greg who'd done all the running after they'd first met. She tried to convince herself this was only carrying on from where they'd left things last night when Joe had started this chain reaction inside her. He'd lit the fuse so he'd have to take responsibility for the fallout.

'I had a good time today.' She stopped short of Miriama's house so they weren't under the porch light and reduced the pressure to make something happen there and then.

'Me too.' Joe's bright smile lit up the semi-darkness and took the chill off the evening air.

She reached out to take the mat from him and Joe brushed his thumb along her fingers in the handover. The only sound she could hear was her own breathing as he watched her intently with no sign of backing away. It was now or never. She swallowed hard as she took a step closer to him.

They were both holding onto the mat as she closed her eyes and offered her lips up to his.

For a heart-stopping moment there was only cold air to meet her. Then the weight of his mouth was on hers, accepting her, loving her and bringing her almost to tears with relief. Each caress of her lips, every flick of his tongue to match hers made her confidence stronger and her body weaker. She'd taken a gamble and this was her reward. In future she'd remember how utterly satisfying, and hot, victory tasted.

It was a triumph over her anxieties, her fears and, above all, her old self. This was anything but boring, as her fevered skin would testify.

'I don't want this.'

Her new fairy wings disappeared and left her plummeting back down to earth as Joe did the one thing she'd feared from the start.

'I, I…' She didn't know whether to apologise or say goodnight but either would be better than dissolving into a puddle of tears, which was exactly what she wanted to do. Her determination to prove she was still attractive to someone, that she could change, had obviously built this up into something Joe hadn't been expecting. The celebrations heralding the brave new Emily had been premature. Nobody wanted *her* either. The difference was she would no longer let other people's opinions define her.

Joe wanted Emily more than anything else in the world right now. That was the problem. It was one thing for him to snatch a kiss from her and walk away but quite another for her to initiate one. Double standards for sure but what was a moment of madness for him could mean something entirely different for her. They were already too close when every attempt to create some distance between them only succeeded in them spending more time together. To what end? She wasn't going to find peace with him when he couldn't find his own.

'Okay, I do want this, there's no point in denying it.' Not when he could see how much hurt he was causing her by doing so. That tilt of the chin didn't fool him when she was clutching her medical bag like a security blanket and her eyes were glassy with tears.

'So why do it? Why keep pretending there isn't something more than my brother or work binding us together?'

He admired her strong stance, facing him out over his cowardice despite her wobbly voice. She deserved the truth. He dug his nails into his palms to stop from reaching out to her. This was exactly why he should have avoided kissing her in the first place.

'I've told you, I'm not boyfriend material. You'll end up just another holiday memory when I move on and after everything you've been through you need more than that. I don't want the level of responsibility that comes with being the rebound guy. I'm not going to be the one to restore your faith in men or be your emotional crutch until you're over Greg, and I won't pretend to be.' Cards on the table, he braced himself for her reaction. He doubted any woman wanted to be told the man they were kissing was emotionally unavailable, and since he hadn't found it in himself to walk away he was counting on her to make that call.

Emily closed the gap he'd created between them. 'I don't remember saying I wanted any of those things from you but thank you for your honesty. I guess we both know where we stand.'

Too close for him to think straight. Alarm bells were ringing in his head with her breathy acceptance of his terms but it was no longer his head he was listening to.

'I don't want this,' he repeated, even as his lips inched towards hers.

'Neither do I.'

Their mouths collided in a crushing kiss as if they were trying to exorcise this need for one another. The very opposite happened to him as his brain short-circuited and erased the reason he shouldn't do this. Something about him being an idiot and Emily accepting it.

The medical bag and mat fell in the dirt as they clung to each other tighter, her hands around his neck, his around her waist, their legs entwined as they tied themselves into a love pretzel, obliterating all pretence for good.

There was so much fire as she came back time and time again for more, exploring him with her tongue, her passion took him completely by surprise. This naked display of desire for him from a woman who worried about every move she made was such an aphrodisiac his body was already racing on to the next stage. Neither of them were ready for that. At least, not here, not now.

He loosened his hold and gradually let the intensity of the embrace subside. Eventually he had to break free before the most demanding part of his anatomy wrestled sole charge of the situation.

'Glad we got that sorted. It stops any future misunderstanding.' The only way he could survive this was to make a joke of it and diffuse the crackling sexual tension for the moment. Neither of them wanted this but it was happening and there was clearly no escape from it on this tiny island.

'Yeah. We wouldn't want things getting awkward at work.' Emily teased him back but she was already collecting her things from the ground, the moment over.

'Goodnight, Emily.' He kissed her on the cheek, avoiding her lips in case his chivalry died altogether.

'Goodnight, Joe,' she whispered directly into his ear.

Even if he hadn't heard it, the deliberately provocative

breathy goodbye would still have had the same effect on his libido. Deadly.

This surge in Emily's confidence had the potential to be one of the greatest challenges of his life if he kept resisting his natural response to her. If she was really the sort of girl who could hook up with a stranger on a whim they'd have got it on as soon as she'd set foot on the beach. The attraction had been there from the start. She'd had no more casual flings than he'd had ex-wives. They were completely incompatible. Except where it counted.

He was a thrill-seeker because he needed that reminder he was still alive, and his life hadn't ended in that blast. There'd been no greater example of that than when he'd had Emily in his arms, his heartbeat thundering in his ears as she'd kissed him.

It would be madness to carry on with this reckless attraction, let it develop beyond stolen kisses in the moonlight and risk anyone getting hurt. Then again, he was an adrenaline junkie. Playing it safe simply wasn't his style and, it would seem, no longer Emily's.

CHAPTER SEVEN

'SOMEONE'S HAPPY THIS MORNING. I heard you up, singing with the birds.' Miriama peered at Emily over the breakfast of sweet rolls she'd provided.

Emily wolfed them down, ravenous after a good night's sleep and some very pleasant dreams.

'I'm loving my time here, that's all,' she said, washing her white lie down with some lemon tea. Whilst she was happy to be here, this morning's mood was solely down to one man on the island.

'And we love having you here. Perhaps you could stay a little while longer?' She had such hope in her eyes it was a shame to let her down. It wasn't everyone who would open their homes up to a complete stranger in the first place and it was lovely for Emily to hear someone wasn't sick of the sight of her. Not yet anyway.

'I wish I could but I've got my own clinic, my own patients, waiting for me at home.' There was no place she'd rather be than Yasi Island right now. It had made quite an impression on her.

She traced the outline of her mouth with her fingertips absent-mindedly, replaying the moment it had all been worth it to come here. It was no wonder Miriama was staring at her as if she was mad. She couldn't stop smiling.

There was no way of telling if it was down to this place

or merely being away from the toxic environment of a life she'd shared with her ex, but she was beginning to feel like a new person. A woman who could override her fears with a burst of courage when it was required. The benefits she'd received in doing so would only inspire her to keep challenging herself.

Until last night she would never have entertained the idea of making a move on a man but she was glad she had. A lovely shiver tickled the back of her neck at the thought of her reward. She didn't know if anything more would come of it and constantly worrying about it would only spoil things. As with any other holiday memory the kiss was simply something to look back on fondly. A fantasy designed to give her a boost when real life became a drudge, not take seriously.

'Oh, well. You're ours for a while at least, so you should go make the most of your time here. I'm sure Joe is waiting for you.'

She tried to block out her inner worrywart, who always did her best to sabotage the good things that came her way, and focus on the positives as she made her way to work. Such as the reserves of courage she hadn't known she'd had to make a move on him in the first place.

'Hey.' Her breakfast did a backflip in her belly at the first Joe sighting of the day.

'Hey,' he said back, every bit as bashful as they faced each other from either end of the hut.

It seemed they were back to yesterday's avoidance tactics again and although it was probably best when they had to work together, there was still that sinking feeling in her stomach that their moment had passed.

They kept themselves busy by setting up what minimal equipment they had and she was glad when Sou made an appearance to interrupt the awkward atmosphere.

'Hey, Sou. What can we do for you?' Joe asked.

'If it's a general health check you want we can start with your blood pressure.' Emily turned back to fetch the blood-pressure cuff, only to collide with that solid wall of muscle again.

'Excuse me,' she said, attempting to duck past Joe.

'Of course.' He moved aside but she promptly ran into him again.

'Sorry.'

'Sorry.'

'If you two have quite finished, is there somewhere I can set these before my arm drops off?' Sou shoved a plate of sweet desserts between Emily and Joe's clumsy tango.

'You can set them over here.' She cleared a space on the table for Sou's offering and prayed it wasn't completely obvious that she and Joe were dealing with personal issues. It was taking all her mental strength to relegate their ten minutes of sexy times to the past when she was still trying to regulate her breathing and her heart rate, but she would never bring her personal business into the workplace.

'I'll go...do something else.' Joe backed out of her personal space and her skittishness immediately began to dissipate.

Good. It would help her get back to the day job if she couldn't see him. They couldn't let things between them affect their work.

'Take a seat, Sou. I wasn't expecting to see you so soon. What can I do for you?'

Yasi Island, and Joe, were making her forget who she was *supposed* to be.

She wrapped the cuff around Sou's upper arm and watched the dial as she inflated it.

'I haven't been myself at all lately and I thought it was about time I saw about it. If I'm honest, it's only because you're here that I'm bothering at all.' Sou rested her hands on her lap and that sparkle she'd had in her eye when she'd first walked in began to dim. There was clearly something bothering her more than she wanted anyone to know.

'Well, your blood pressure's fine. We'll start with taking a few measurements and then we'll discuss whatever problems you're having.' Emily unfastened the cuff and started a file for her new patient. She plotted her height on the wall chart and pushed the scales out to get a quick weight reading.

Sou was fifty-eight, and very overweight, which could lead to all manner of health issues.

'I'm tired and thirsty all the time. I know I'm not getting any younger but I'm exhausted.'

'Are you passing urine more frequently too?' Alarm bells were already ringing in her doctor brain.

'I thought that was because of the extra drinks?'

'It could be but we have to look into all possibilities. Tell me, Sou, do you know if there's a history of diabetes in your family?' It would certainly explain the symptoms but Emily didn't have the means to treat it effectively here. She would have to refer Sou to hospital on the mainland for the kind of long-term care that would require and she'd have to be certain of her diagnosis before she started the ball rolling on that score.

'My mother had it but she hated the hospital. She didn't always do everything they advised. She was a stubborn lady and I miss her.' The fear in her voice came from someone who didn't want to follow that same path but neither did she want to face the scary truth. It was important for Emily to treat her with kid gloves so she didn't scare her off back into denial.

'If it is diabetes we're dealing with, we *can* manage it effectively. First things first. We'll do a wee sample to test your blood sugar levels. You'll feel a little prick in your finger as the needle draws the blood but it'll all be over in seconds. Okay?' She only had the small reading device at her disposal and any in-depth analysis would have to be done in the hospital labs but it should give her a good indication if there was a problem.

Sou nodded her head and slowly extended her hand. While Emily was used to this sort of test she understood this wasn't something her patient would be too familiar with and counted to three before she clicked the needle into the skin.

Unfortunately her hunch proved correct. The glucose levels exceeded those she'd hoped for.

'Going by the reading here, diabetes is a definite possibility. I'd like to repeat the test tomorrow if you could fast in the morning for me. We'll take a urine sample first thing too to make sure this isn't some sort of anomaly. If there's no change we're going to have to refer you to the hospital to arrange long-term care for the condition.'

She rested her hand on Sou's, wishing this lovely woman had better news coming to her. 'You can do a little something to help yourself in the meantime. If you could cut out the sweet stuff and take up even the smallest exercise, it can make all the difference.'

Sou's long stare was that of a woman who may as well have been handed a death sentence. Emily understood how much food was a part of the culture here but Sou needed to help herself when there wasn't immediate access to medical facilities and drugs on the island. Diabetes unchecked could lead to all sorts of other health complications, which were often more difficult to treat. Prevention was always better than cure.

'We can work together to come up with a healthy eating plan if it would help.'

'Yes, please.'

That would be her homework tonight, to try and devise a meal plan that could work in a place where food supplies were already limited. With any luck Joe would help her. Putting their heads together for the sake of their patients was the perfect excuse to cosy up this evening.

'I know it's easier said than done but try not to worry about it. Carry on as normal tonight. We'll do more tests tomorrow, then take it from there.' She'd get his advice on hospital referrals too when he'd finished with his own patient. Joni was currently monopolising his time with another sports injury of some sort.

'Can I still drink kava?'

If this had been a patient at home she wouldn't be encouraging alcohol but not overwhelming Sou with too much change was just as important. They'd take this one step at a time together.

'I'm not going to stop you partaking tonight but we will look into your alcohol intake as part of this lifestyle change at some point. Everything's possible in moderation. Now, go home, talk this over with Tomasi and I'll see you back here in the morning.'

Sou rose slowly from the bed. It was no wonder she was still in a daze after the bombshell she'd just had dropped on her.

'I'm here any time you need to talk or if you have any questions.'

'Thanks, Emily.'

'No problem. We'll get you back to your old self as soon as we can.' She wrapped Sou in a bear hug, another thing she'd never have dreamed of doing in her own practice. That line between patient and friend had been blurred around the same time as the one with Joe.

She made a note to call in and check on Sou later as she waved her off. It was a lot for her to take in and meant huge changes in her life, something that was always difficult to come to terms with even when it was for the best. She was a prime example herself of someone who'd resisted adapting to the new hand fate had dealt her and was only now reaping the benefits of that evolution. It would've been nice if she'd had someone to hold her hand and assure her things would be okay and her world wouldn't come to an end because of one event.

Perhaps she wouldn't have been in the right head space to hear those platitudes about life going on after Greg but it had, and in quite dramatic fashion. In those dark early days she'd never have imagined flying to a remote island, treating patients with rudimentary equipment and snogging the local totty. She was proud of herself for all of it. Sou would be too if she made a few simple changes to improve her lot. Although Joe was definitely out of bounds, she would find her courage rewarded in other ways.

Her attention inevitably returned to her army medic, who was patching up Joni's knee. She could hear the pair of them laughing and was automatically drawn towards the easy camaraderie after the difficult start to the day.

'Have you been in the wars again?' she asked the patient, who was lying on the bed with his hands behind his head as relaxed as could be.

'The perils of running and not paying attention.' Joe grinned at her over his shoulder, sending her pulse skipping off into the sunset with her common sense.

'It's as well you're made of tough stuff around here, huh?' Her attempt at playful banter fell flat as Joni was staring at her unblinkingly, clearly disturbed by her presence.

He sat up, his face screwed up as he peered closer into her face, his nose wrinkled in disgust. Emily moved away from the bedside taken aback by the boy's sudden change in demeanour. She could sense Joe tensing next to her too and she panicked she'd made a mistake in coming over and interrupting their male bonding.

'What happened to your face, Doc?'

It was the kind of blunt questioning she should've been used to by now but it still managed to knock the air out of her lungs. This was why she took great steps to make sure she kept her birthmark covered and avoid this sort of confrontation. Joni had reacted so strongly there had to be something wrong with her usually foolproof camouflage.

She'd been so high on life this morning she barely remembered anything before coming to work. Her routine never differed—shower, dress, make-up, breakfast. Except this wasn't any ordinary day and this certainly wasn't the usual running order. She'd swapped her hot showers for buckets of cold water, dressed according to the weather instead of her job title, and…she didn't recall performing her twenty-minute beauty regime while she'd been singing and daydreaming about the night before. That would teach her to get carried away with romance. Now stark reality was staring her right in the face. This fairy-tale was well and truly over.

'I…uh…' She scrabbled around for her bag. There should be an emergency compact in there and she'd handle this better if she wasn't so exposed.

She couldn't even look at Joe now her big secret had been revealed in its full gory glory. Goodness knew what he was thinking. Probably how much of a lucky escape he'd had.

'It's a birthmark. Just a different coloured patch of skin Emily was born with. We're lucky she feels comfortable enough with us to stop hiding it under her make-up.' Joe shot her a smile warm enough to thaw out her bones, which were chilled after being called out on her deception. Bless him, he was trying to make this easy on her when he'd been the one kept in the dark.

She was torn now between doing a last-minute cover-up, pretending this had never happened, or playing along that this had been a deliberate move on her part. Joe wasn't stupid, he'd have known she'd never have intentionally 'come out' and left herself open to such scrutiny. It was testament to his strength of character for trying to save her blushes when it must have been a shock to his system to see her like this. Greg wouldn't have been so accommodating. He would've escorted her to the nearest mirror to rectify her glaring blunder. Although he wouldn't have let her leave the house make-up-free in the first place, never mind make excuses for her. He'd always made her feel as though she earned more respect from people when she perpetuated the lie about her true appearance.

She was lucky to have met a man who didn't need to put her down and always did his best to make her comfortable in her surroundings. No matter what the circumstances. That total acceptance of her as a person was something rare in her world.

'Does it hurt?' Joni was still staring at her face, which was aflame with the continued line of questioning.

'No. I forget it's even there.' That wasn't strictly true. Apart from today when it had apparently gone completely out of her head, that wretched port wine stain was the bane of her existence.

It was a boring enough answer for the child to lose interest.

'Will I have a scar?' he asked as Joe finished dressing his knee.

'No. You should be all healed up in a day or two. Now, get yourself off to school before your teacher sends out a search party for you.'

Joni looked remarkably disappointed not to have a long-lasting reminder of his injury as he hopped down off the bed. 'I suppose I'll see you later, then.'

At least when he was engrossed in his own woes it stopped him gawping at her as though she was a sideshow attraction. The novelty usually wore off but that initial shock and revulsion was always difficult to stomach. Sometimes children could be the worst, laughing and pointing at her affliction, too young to understand the pain it would cause, but Joni had been quite straightforward about the matter. He'd asked questions and once they'd been answered it was no longer an issue. He'd made no judgement on her as a person because of her physical disfigurement.

It suddenly struck her that Sou and Miriama had also seen her without her camouflage. That explained the curious stares that she'd put down to her Joe-enhanced mood but they'd just been too polite to comment.

A woman with a dark red birthmark apparently wasn't anything the people of Yasi were going to waste energy thinking about when they were working so hard to just get by themselves. Physical attractiveness didn't hold much meaning out here because it had no effect on their quality of life. That's the way it should be; the way Emily preferred it. Except when she was unashamedly ogling Joe, of course. She was aware of the irony.

Joe. He'd seen her long before Sou or Joni had come onto the scene and he hadn't blinked, hadn't felt the need to point it out to her.

She opened her mouth, trying to find the words she needed to express what that meant to her, and failing. His easy acceptance was already making her tear up.

'Is everything all right with Sou? I think Joni was only trying to avoid class. He spends so much time here we should probably find him a job.'

She couldn't believe he wasn't even going to mention her birthmark. Honestly, she was finding his nonchalance even more disturbing than the boy's reaction. It wasn't the norm and, as such, she didn't know how to handle it.

In the end she decided to go with honesty and straight

talking. Another new first when it came to relationships for her.

'Are you really going to stand there and pretend nothing's wrong?'

'What are you talking about?' His naivety on the subject was annoying her now. No one could possibly be that oblivious to her predicament.

'This.' She couldn't believe she was voluntarily pointing out her flaw.

'Oh, your birthmark? I see it. So what?' He shrugged, increasing the chances of her giving him a good shake.

'So what, he says. You could have given me a heads up I'd gone out in public like this.' She didn't know why she was taking her mistake out on him when he'd been nothing but supportive. Her lashing out might have had something to do with this being the most vulnerable she'd felt since arriving on the island.

'As I said to Joni, I'd assumed you were actually comfortable enough around us to stop hiding away.'

'You weren't shocked? I mean, this ugly big mess can take some getting used to.' Nearly thirty years of living with it hadn't made it any easier for her so she didn't expect anyone else to take it in their stride the way Joe had.

'If I'm honest, I knew about it. I've seen the family photos Peter carries around with him but even if I hadn't it doesn't make any difference to me.'

Emily had to admit that took the shine off his brilliance somewhat. He'd had time to prepare himself for the great revelation. Unlike her discovery about his hearing problem. Perhaps the knowledge of her struggles with defective body parts had been what had drawn him to her in the first place and had made her seem attractive as another damaged soul. If something appeared too good to be true, it usually was.

'Hey. Your birthmark is part of you. How could it be

anything other than beautiful?' He tilted her chin up so she had to look in his eyes and believe what she saw there—pure, undiluted desire.

Whether he'd had advance warning or not, whether she covered up or not, he always looked at her as though she was the sexiest woman alive. There was no greater compliment for a woman like her. When he'd said her birthmark didn't matter to him, holding her gaze this way, she was more inclined to believe it.

Joe leaned forward and placed a light kiss on the exact spot between her cheek and her nose where her greatest weakness blazed brightly. She held her breath. It was one of those moments she'd dreamed of, when someone would embrace her, warts and all, not shy away from any part of her. She'd never had that complete acceptance from Greg and, despite being together so long, she'd always been slightly on edge. With good reason, it had turned out.

Joe was different. He believed in qualities and causes that mattered, not superficial nonsense that held no significant meaning. He was a special person. One with whom her time was limited.

Typical.

If she was only to encounter this kind of acceptance once in her lifetime she should really immerse herself in the experience. No holding back. No regrets. Be herself without conditions.

For the first time in her life she was seriously considering ditching her camouflage on a permanent basis and really letting loose. It was a bold move she would never have undertaken without Joe's unconditional support, and she was keen to share the rest of the adventure with him.

CHAPTER EIGHT

THERE WERE TIMES when Joe needed his medical work to give his life meaning and other times it was something he felt compelled to do. Today it felt like the latter. He'd volunteered to come to Yasi because he'd genuinely wanted to help, and he still did, but the success of the clinic had curtailed his personal life. That hadn't been a problem up until now. He'd spent all day treating one patient after another with Emily almost within arm's reach. It was torture if he was expected to forget everything that had happened between them.

He shouldn't complain, though, when their outreach yesterday had garnered so many follow-up appointments. It would go a long way towards improving the long-term health of the inhabitants. At one point they'd had a queue outside of people waiting to be seen for check-ups, which hadn't happened since he'd set up the clinic. Such an influx could've been overwhelming for Emily, especially since she'd chosen not to cover up her birthmark again. Of course there'd been comments and stares but she'd dealt with them all without any upset or drama, as if she'd reconciled herself about living without the make-up.

When she'd turned up this morning, her natural beauty shining through, all he'd wanted to do was take her in his arms and kiss her. It didn't matter it had turned out to have been an oversight on her part, her actions since had established her bravery and made him want her more. Every inadvertent brush against each other since had simply increased his desire to act on that impulse—impossible given their circumstances, not to mention the room full of people between them for most of the day. He couldn't afford to let anyone else down when he was still coming to terms with the last time he'd failed people who had needed his help.

They were making a difference here and that's what was important. Along with minor ailments and a test of his suturing skills on one of the local craftsmen, who'd whittled his hand instead of the wood he was supposed to be carving, they'd uncovered a few more serious health issues in the older population. Emily had confided in him about Sou, but diabetes, along with hypertension, wasn't an uncommon problem in remote regions like Yasi. Without adequate primary health care access and education, the rates of non-communicable diseases were often high and many cardiovascular risk factors also went unchecked. He already had a list of patients who'd require further investigation and treatment in proper hospital facilities.

In turn, the island was also doing Emily the power of good. That creep of an ex-husband had taken a sledgehammer to her confidence with his callous behaviour but she was flourishing out here. The same woman who forty-eight hours ago had been unable to walk more than twenty paces without touching up her make-up and had wanted to hide from company was fresh-faced and joking about with the locals.

She'd told all manner of tall tales to explain the birthmark, making light of it to avoid any awkwardness. He'd even heard her tell one curious patient it was the result of dodgy suncream application. By the time she revealed the truth it didn't seem to matter any more. Talking about it somehow made it less of a big deal and it was great to see Emily comfortable in her own skin. She didn't need him to wrap her in cotton wool when she was making such great progress on her own. It made his life easier too if she wasn't relying on him to act as intermediary any more.

'I've got another patient to add to the list of referrals. His heartbeat is irregular and he's out of breath. I'd be happier if he had an ECG to see what's going on in there.' Emily was all business as she approached him during a lull. She'd wound her hair up into a topknot and Joe's hand twitched to reach out and pluck out the pen holding it in place.

He gave himself a shake to rid himself of the image of her shaking her hair loose and showed her he could be just as professional. 'If you jot down all his details I'm going to make a few calls on the satellite phone later to the medical outreach co-ordinator and the hospital to get people here as soon as possible. Perhaps they can arrange communal transport to save money and effort in the transfer.'

'Like a community day trip? I suppose they could take a picnic and do some sightseeing on the way.' The corner of her mouth curved up as she teased him.

'Careful or I'll appoint you as tour rep.'

'I'd say you're the man for the job, not me. I imagine you'd be really good.'

He knew she was referring to the introductions he'd made for her around the island, yet the unintended innuendo immediately brought a groan from his inner Neanderthal. Given the chance with Emily he'd show her just how good he could be.

Her cheeks flushed scarlet as though she was reading his X-rated thoughts. The only thing more frustrating than not being able to act on his attraction to Emily was being aware that she wanted him too.

She made a move towards the new batch of patients hovering nearby, but Joe was finding it hard to let the moment pass without recognising the frisson of sexual energy they'd created in the space of a few seconds. Despite the buzz and whirr of the neon danger signs around her, he enjoyed Emily's company and the adrenaline rush he got simply from being around her.

He leaned down to whisper in her ear as she passed by. 'Why don't we get together tonight?'

Her eyes nearly popped out of her head at the suggestion. Clearly her thoughts were as muddled as his own about his motives. 'I, er…'

'You know, to catch up on that patient transfer list.' They could play it safe, didn't have to do anything other than chat about their working day. It would be novelty enough for him to entertain a guest, without getting into trouble with Peter's sibling and causing all manner of problems.

'Oh, yes. Of course. I'd also appreciate your help in devising some sort of healthy eating plan for Sou. We could even draw up an easy-to-read guide on healthier living for everyone to explain the basics.'

'Why don't we do it over dinner?'

'Here?'

'Sure. Leave it with me. As soon as we wrap up here you go and get freshened up and I'll rustle up some food for us. Just a quiet dinner for two.' So far, all their meals had been very public affairs where she'd found it difficult to relax. He wanted to change that for her without the pressure of structured proceedings. Just work talk and chill.

'That would be nice.'

'So it's a date, then?' He couldn't stop himself from teasing her one last time.

'It's a date,' she confirmed, before resuming her work

duties. The smile on her face eased the sense of loss as she turned away, knowing he'd been the one to put it there.

He had no expectations for anything beyond a nice evening together. A working dinner sounded more manageable for both of them long-term than an appointment for hot, unforgettable sex. Although he imagined that's exactly what would happen if they ever gave in to temptation.

That thought wasn't going to help this day go any faster.

The butterflies in her stomach might be older and more cynical than they had been fifteen years ago when she'd gone on her first date to the cinema, but they weren't any less mobile on this *non-date*. She was playing with fire tonight and she knew it. Joe had made it clear he didn't intend anything other than work-related conversation, but their apparent chemistry had a way of throwing them off track. She took full responsibility for last night's descent into madness and she wasn't ashamed of it. Taking the initiative had given her a confidence boost, especially when he'd been so responsive to her advances, but she wasn't sure she wanted to take things any further than that. Joe was an experienced man of the world who'd invariably expect more than a kiss in the moonlight.

Although she'd initially been disappointed they hadn't carried on where they'd left off, it was probably better they let things cool off. As much as she wanted to exorcise her demons once and for all, she wasn't ready to sleep with anyone yet, not even someone who was so accepting of her, flaws and all. While the idea of sharing Joe's bed was appealing on the surface, it would probably only give her more issues to worry about. Including all the ways in which he could find her lacking as a lover, given her limited experience.

Until she fully overcame her personal issues she'd have

to make do with the exhilaration of anticipation instead. This was the most alive she'd felt since the divorce, when all hope inside her for the future had seemed to have died along with her marriage. Even the idea he might want to sleep with her had definitely got the blood pumping back in her veins and that was enough for now.

She'd come armed as she entered the battlefield tonight where hormones would fight against her battered heart for supremacy. Flowers and chocolates were usually the gifts to bring on such an auspicious occasion but stationery was her particular weapon of choice this evening. An armful of paper, glue and coloured markers seemed like a good distraction from the beds that would dominate tonight's dinner venue.

She'd informed Miriama she'd be working late and wouldn't be around for supper when she'd gone back to change. There wasn't much to choose from in her limited wardrobe but she'd gone with Capri pants and a navy and white polka-dot halterneck for what she hoped was a touch of vintage glamour. It had taken longer for her decide on her make-up for the evening. While using her thick foundation could be seen as taking a step backwards, there weren't many women who'd get ready for an evening in male company without a little extra help. After much debate she'd decided a sweep of mascara over her eyelashes and a dab of lip-gloss would do just fine.

She'd taken so much time and care over her appearance she hadn't given a thought to how Joe would look tonight. When he opened the door to her she hadn't expected to see him in anything other than his casual T-shirt and shorts combo. So the more formal cream-coloured linen trousers and unbuttoned white shirt he was rocking had her eyes out on stalks.

'What? You don't think I can scrub up well too?'

'You look great.' She appreciated the effort he'd gone

to for her and that appreciation had reached deep inside and touched somewhere that definitely went beyond the friendship realm.

'So do you.' He leaned in to give her a welcome peck on the cheek, his skin smooth against hers and smelling of aftershave and soap.

She closed her eyes and breathed him in, the combination of familiar citrus tones and spicy musk seeming to complement his personality perfectly. Like him, his cologne was comforting with a dangerous hint of the exotic. Not to mention so very moreish. But standing on the doorstep, sniffing him, wasn't supposed to be the highlight of her evening.

'I'm intrigued to find out what you have planned for dinner.' She didn't have much of an appetite, at least not for food, but she was curious about how he'd sourced it, or if he'd cooked it himself.

'Come in and be prepared to be blown away. I can guarantee you the best meal you've had on the island, all cooked by my own fair hand.' He ushered her inside with the urgency of a man keen to show off said cooking skills.

'Bold claims. You're going to have to go a long way to top Sou's spread last night. I hope you've had some training.' She was still battling her fear of new foods, especially when not all of them here were to her taste. Except the coconut spinach thing.

Please, let it be the coconut spinach thing.

'I'll have you know I've cooked this very same meal while trekking through the Amazon rainforest. I'm a very capable chef who has whipped up a veritable feast even in the most trying circumstances.'

'In that case, I'm most honoured to be your guest.' And impressed with the casual mention of what must have been the most epic of adventures. Time spent in the jungle put her island escape well and truly in the shade.

Conditions here were probably luxurious compared to what he'd endured and she was panicking about what was on the menu. She should think herself lucky people were happy to keep feeding her. If left to her own devices she'd probably starve once her biscuit stash ran out.

'Take a seat and make yourself comfortable. You can set your things over there in the corner.'

She thought it was his idea of a joke when her bones were still protesting against this tradition of sitting on hard wood floors until she saw what he'd done with the place. The room was lit with the lanterns she'd seen in all the other houses, which somehow here they took on that air of intimacy a candlelit dinner for two demanded. He'd pushed all the medical equipment to the side and pulled the table, now covered with one of the painted *masa* mats, into the middle of the room. There were even two crude wooden chairs, one either side of the makeshift dining table. Bliss!

'I thought we were doing paperwork.' She clutched her armful of stationery closer. It was her security blanket, supposed to keep her grounded and stop her from getting carried away with the idea of romance.

'We are but we'll think better on a full stomach.' He eased the supplies from her grasp and set them on top of the medicine cabinet.

'It might be an idea to make a food pyramid to explain the basic principles of healthy living at a glance. You know, one of those colour-coded posters that starts with a small amounts of fatty foods bad for the body and ends with encouraging more fruit and veg in the diet.'

'Sure. I'm no artist but I'm sure we can manage a simple pictograph between us. Now, if you'll excuse me I must go and check on dinner cooking on my camping stove out the back.' It was only when he padded away from her that Emily noticed he was barefoot. He had his very own brand of sophistication that, while traditionally handsome, still paid homage to his bohemian nature. The best of both worlds from a spectator's point of view.

He gave a half-bow before ducking back outside. Emily took the seat facing the door in order to see this spectacle as it unfolded. He'd certainly gone to a lot of trouble but nothing so far indicated what she should expect on her plate. Her suspense was prolonged even further when dinner did arrive as he kept it covered, using an upturned wooden bowl as an improvised cloche.

'Ta-da!' He lifted the cover with a flourish.

Emily released the breath she'd been holding in a splutter of disbelief. 'Beans on toast? Where on earth did you get that?'

The welcome sight of an old British favourite, baked beans in tomato sauce, was a little piece of home that immediately brought her comfort. He'd even taken the care to toast the rustic bread to keep it authentic.

'We explorers always carry a few emergency supplies.' He produced an empty tin, which he'd obviously brought with him from England.

'This beats a fancy restaurant any day of the week.'

'Wait. You haven't seen anything yet.' He disappeared again, returning with two tin cups full of what looked suspiciously like English tea.

She took a sip of sweet heaven. 'But how…?'

Joe sat down too. 'I told you, I have a few essentials and I called in a few favours for the rest.'

She wanted to tell him he shouldn't have gone to so much trouble for her but she was too grateful to him for sacrificing his supplies for her. And her mouth was watering to taste something familiar.

'I've never eaten beans and toast with my fingers.'

'You don't have to. Unless you want to.' He reached into his pocket and pulled out a set of small stainless-steel cutlery. The kind no good Boy Scout would ever leave home without. It also proved his commitment to being part of the community here when he'd chosen to forgo using them until now.

Emily reached out and snatched a knife and fork from him. 'It's the little things that mean the most.'

That first bite of hearty nostalgia seemed to go in slow motion as she savoured the taste of home, enjoying the textures and flavours she knew so well. After that, she practically devoured her plate in hunger. When she was done she wiped her chin to make sure she hadn't embarrassed herself by dripping tomato sauce down herself.

'I aim to please.' He set down his cutlery on his clean plate with every reason to look smug after pulling out all the stops tonight. She wouldn't have been more pleased if he'd wined and dined her at The Ritz.

'I can't believe you did this. More to the point, I can't believe you wore white, knowing this was what we were eating. That's a laundry nightmare waiting to happen.'

He leaned forward, his intense gaze holding her captive in her seat, that desire they'd been trying to swerve all day flaring back into life. 'What can I say? I live right on the edge of danger.'

They both did if the sparks between them were anything to go by.

'Maybe we should get started on our craft project?' Before they cleared the table and lunged at each other in a fit of passion.

'There's no rush. Now, I hope you have room for dessert?'

'Always.' It was usually her favourite part of a meal but there wasn't much that could possibly top that main course.

Except the two chocolate bars he was waving in her face. All her Christmases had come at once.

'I was saving them for a special occasion.'

'Well, now's not the time to be selfish,' she said, holding out a hand for her share, secretly pleased he deemed an evening in her company 'special' when she was thinking exactly the same thing about him.

He was good-looking, generous, thoughtful and funny. Everything a woman could want in a man.

Joe Braden spelled trouble with a capital 'T'.

'Hmm, I don't think I'll ever make it as an artist.' Emily chewed the end of her pen and squinted at her depiction of Fijian desserts in the 'Eat Less' section at the top of the food pyramid. The only reason she didn't feel a hypocrite after scoffing down that chocolate was because it was the only indulgence she'd had in three days.

After their feast on comfort foods they'd got their heads together to create a diet plan for Sou and had now taken up residence on the floor to work on their healthy eating poster. The idea that there'd be more room to spread out had actually led to the two of them sitting almost on top of each other as they drew on the same piece of paper.

Joe glanced up from his scribbling to see her efforts for himself. 'Don't put yourself down. That's an excellent cheese wedge.'

'It's supposed to be coconut cake.'

'Maybe we should label everything.'

She gave him a dig with her elbow, making him give his perfectly drawn apple an extra-long stalk on the 'Eat More' shelf as he laughed at his own joke.

'I think they'll get the gist of the message and we'll explain it as part of the general physical exam anyway.'

'I'm only messing with you. I reckon we've done a great job. This artwork will still be hanging here displaying the info long after we've gone, essentially doing our

job in our absence.' Joe hammered his fist on the sheet of
A4 paper in passionate defence of their initiative.

'That's a scary thought,' she said with a giggle. He did
make her laugh. And swoon.

'Which bit? The quality of our legacy or the idea of us
leaving this place?'

Just like that the jovial mood gave way to something
more serious, something more intense. Leaving Yasi
meant leaving Joe behind too and she wasn't ready for
that. He held her gaze and right there and then she knew
she didn't want this to be over. She wanted this to be the
beginning.

'Both.'

It was impossible to tell who'd made the first move
when they'd both leaned in for the kiss.

Joe fastened his lips to hers with such stunning conviction she knew he'd been waiting for this too. She was
starting to forget why she shouldn't let this happen when
he knew her secret already and embraced it with more
passion than she'd ever expected. He hadn't looked at her
with any kind of pity today, only desire. Unless he was
a very good actor or did charity work as a self-esteem
booster for unfortunates, he didn't seem bothered by her
au naturel appearance.

She scooted closer to deepen their connection and sample the best course of the evening in her opinion. Kissing him was even better than chocolate but every bit as
delicious. Every romantic bone in her body melted as
he pulled her close and reached out to cup her face in
his hands, possessing her completely. It could've been a
scene taken directly from one of those over-sentimental
chick flicks she'd overindulged in recently. It was perfect.

Too perfect, that small voice of doom piped up.

It wasn't real; they weren't going to run off into the
sunset together at the end of this.

Shut up, Miss Stick-in-the-Mud, and let me enjoy my wild side for once.

While the inner debate went on in her head, her body was making the next move for her. With her arms snaked around his neck and the rest of her draped over him like a silk scarf she was getting the full Joe Braden experience. He was all hard lines and smooth planes, the ideal structure to support her melty bones. They fitted together so well, felt so natural together, she didn't know why she'd worried so much. This dance around each other since her arrival had only been delaying the inevitable and they didn't have much time left together to waste. From now on she was going to take his advice and go with the flow, whatever direction it carried her.

Emily's knees were sliding from under her as he lowered her back onto the floor; their project quickly becoming a victim of their desire beneath their entangled limbs. Joe's body was heavy against hers but she'd never felt more secure, either with herself or another. Despite all her earlier anxieties, anticipating this moment, there was nowhere she'd rather be than here lying with him.

That didn't mean she wasn't a little skittish. She gasped at that first intimate touch as Joe slid his hand under her top to caress her breast, the skin-on-skin contact a shock to her system after all this time.

'You okay?' He immediately withdrew, leaving her feeling cold without the warmth of his touch.

'Mmm-hmm.' She nodded, keen to reconnect before she lost her bottle. It was better if she didn't have time to overthink and when his hands were on her she couldn't think about anything other than how good he made her feel.

'Tell me if this is going too fast,' he whispered against her neck, nuzzling that sensitive skin and stealing any potential argument from her.

'No.' Her breathy impatience saw him seek her out once more, kneading that soft mound into a hardened peak. Far from her usual cautious nature, she wanted to throw herself completely into the moment. She was too busy *feeling* to think or worry and it made her positively wanton, grinding her body against Joe's, aching for more.

His shirt came away easily beneath her busy fingers to reveal the well-defined torso she'd only ogled from afar until now. Up close it was even more impressive as she slid her hands over the bumps and contours of his body. It was amazing that one man was in possession of so much inner and outer beauty and she counted herself lucky she got to experience all of it.

The cool air puckered her nipple ever harder as Joe exposed her fully to his gaze. And his tongue. She moaned and arched up off the floor as he drove her to the brink of insanity with every flick. That little bud seemed to contain every nerve ending in her body, tightened with complete arousal and straining for his touch.

Eyes closed as she surrendered to her needs, she let her hands survey the rest of Joe's body. They slipped easily along his smooth skin until they met that trail of hair leading into the waistband of his trousers. Suddenly her nakedness didn't matter as much as his. She wanted to see all of him, feel all of him pressed against her. Into her.

He sucked in a breath as she unfastened the button and dared to go ever lower to trace the hard ridge of his erection. It was her turn to gasp. There was no denying the strength of his desire for her when the steely evidence was right there beneath her fingertips. The knowledge that the flawed Emily still had the ability to turn him on to this extent was a powerful motivator.

She explored his length and self-control through the fabric of his briefs, enjoying the groans of pleasure and frustration she drew from him with every feathery stroke along his shaft. However, teasing him also meant she was testing the limits of her own restraint and she was never one to inflict unnecessary pain on herself.

She squeezed his taut backside and Joe closed his eyes and tilted his head back in ecstasy. This shameless need to follow her desire and to hell with the consequences was new, exciting, and though she wanted to reach that final peak she didn't want this feeling to end. Although she might spontaneously combust if they didn't bring this to its natural conclusion soon.

She was scrabbling to undo the zip on her own trousers when the door burst open.

'We need your help!'

Emily screamed.

Joe swore.

'Get out!' he shouted, throwing himself on top of her to save what was left of her modesty.

'I'm sorry. Holy—'

She didn't hear the rest as the door closed again but she imagined there was probably an expletive missing at the end of the sentence.

'Was that—?'

'Yeah,' Joe confirmed her worst fears as he leaned his forehead on her chest and swore again.

The best moment of her life had transformed into one of the worst. Her own stepbrother had just walked in on her about to have sex with his best friend.

Lying here half-undressed with an almost naked Joe spread-eagled across the top of her suddenly became tawdry when she viewed it from Peter's perspective. The cold dose of reality brought back all the reasons this should have remained nothing more than a bad idea.

'I need to get up.' She pushed Joe off and covered herself up again, the thrill of the evening well and truly having worn off. It was unfortunate that after everything she'd gone through to reach this point she was back to being a disappointment.

Emily was hunched over, hugging her knees and almost rocking with the trauma of having Peter catch them at it on the floor. Joe knew he was going to have to man up and face the consequences with her stepbrother. The thought of that had killed his arousal stone-dead.

Once he'd relocated his shirt and pulled his trousers back up, he crouched down beside her.

'We didn't do anything wrong,' he whispered, desperate for her to come back to him. They'd acted on their mutual attraction, not committed a crime.

'I know.' She said it so softly and with so little conviction he'd had to read her lips. He could see the shame clouding her face and curling her body into a ball.

If it had been anybody else who'd burst in uninvited he would've read them the Riot Act, but on this occasion Peter had claim on the victim role. He needed to go and do some damage control but he was reluctant to leave Emily there, reflecting on the embarrassment she'd been subjected to because of him. He should've taken better care of her.

He dipped his head to drop a kiss on her lips, hoping to keep that connection alive. They'd come this far and risked so much to get to this point that it would be a shame to take two steps back now, but she remained motionless, unresponsive to the gesture. This sudden impassiveness wasn't something he was simply going to accept after the fire he'd just witnessed from her. He wanted her to stay with him and not give in to unnecessary guilt. She'd had enough of that recently.

With her face cradled in his hands, he teased her lips apart with the tip of his tongue, searching for that woman who'd had her hands down his pants not five minutes ago. Slowly but surely she began to respond, tentatively meeting his tongue with hers and opening her mouth to invite him further. He wanted to scoop her up and carry her off somewhere peaceful and private, preferably with carpet on the floor and a king-size bed. They needed somewhere with no distractions, no outside influences interfering in how they expressed their feelings for one another. Emotionally they mightn't have it all figured out, but until Peter had arrived they'd been happy for their bodies to make their decisions for them.

The sound of banging on the door reverberated around the room.

'Guys, I know this is…er…bad timing but we really have an emergency out here. So if you could postpone this for now and get your clothes on, I'd really appreciate it.' Peter was shouting so loudly it wasn't hard to figure out what he thought of this match. Seeing Joe rolling around half-naked with his stepsister might have played a part in colouring that judgement.

'We have to go. Peter definitely wouldn't be hanging around unless he really had to. It must be serious.' It was Emily who finally became the voice of reason. Someone needed their help, and everything else would have to wait.

Joe was dreading coming face-to-face with Peter more than whatever crisis was going on beyond this one.

'Are we good?' He wanted confirmation before they took this outside.

Emily nodded and attempted a smile. It would have to do until they were alone again and able to speak freely.

There was no putting this off any longer. They couldn't afford to let any awkwardness take precedence over someone's health. Joe opened the door to a scowling Peter.

'It's the chief's son. You'd better come and see him.' He turned on his heel, barely able to look at either of them.

Joe could hardly blame him. He was lucky he hadn't been on the receiving end of a fist. Although there was

still time. He quickened his pace to keep up with his probably now ex-mate, aware that Emily was content to hang
back.

'What's wrong with him?'

'He's running a fever, vomiting, and generally in a really bad way.'

In this region there was always a chance those symptoms could be more serious than a run-of-the-mill stomach bug. Malaria, typhoid and dengue fever were also
commonplace alongside the usual culprits. They were
also potentially deadly. He'd seen them all on his travels,
along with the variable outcomes.

Joe stopped abruptly.

'We'll need medical supplies if he's too weak to come
here for treatment.' It was the first thing he should have
checked before heading off, and showed how far his focus
had strayed over the course of the evening. This wasn't
a typical nine-to-five job where he could clock off and
have romantic nights in when he felt like it.

'Of course. There's no way he'd make it back here.'
Peter slowed too as if he should also take the blame for
the oversight. They were obviously all a little shaken up
and not thinking as rationally as they should in their rush
to get away from the scene of the alleged crime.

'I'll go back and get them,' Emily piped up from the
back.

'Pardon me?' He wasn't sure he'd heard her correctly.
Volunteering to go back meant she would have to find
her way out to the chief's house alone, in the dark. It was
a clear sign how much she was dreading being left with
her stepbrother, trying to make conversation. He wasn't
looking forward to it much himself.

'I said I'll get what we need and meet you both out
there.' She spoke louder, with a determination he couldn't
very well object to.

'Will you be able to find your way in the dark?' It was one thing for two ex-soldiers who'd been living here for weeks to track their way back with very little illumination and quite another for Emily, who was still getting to know her way around.

'I'll be fine. I'll grab a lantern from the clinic.'

Oh, yeah, that made sense. He might have done that himself if he hadn't thought he'd need both hands to fend off an irate stepbrother. Peter was keeping it together for now but he knew him well enough to know that rage was bubbling somewhere under that apparently calm surface.

'We're probably going to need antibiotics, paracetamol, a blood-pressure cuff, maybe an IV line—'

'I'm sure I can handle it.' Emily wasted no more time as she spun round and walked towards the light coming from the clinic.

He'd been so busy trying to cover all possibilities he'd neglected to give her any credit as his medically qualified equal in the process. That was another member of the Jackson family he was going to have to try and make amends with later. It wasn't that he was *trying* to tick everyone off tonight, it had simply happened organically.

'You heard her. We'll go on without her.' There was the tone of a big brother/kid sister talk waiting to happen and it wasn't as if Joe could walk away and let them get on with it. He was very much a part of it.

'Mate, I know what that must've looked like.' He was literally cringing at having to remind Peter of what he'd just witnessed but he didn't want to ignore the obvious tension and have their friendship fester because of it.

'Unless I'm wrong, it looked like you were seducing my sister on the floor.' Peter's teeth were a glistening vision of naked aggression in the moonlight and Joe braced himself for imminent attack.

'You're partially right. Although I wouldn't have said

it was all one-sided. Emily's a woman who knows her own mind—'

'I don't want to know the details, thanks.'

'Right. I just mean we both like each other. We're having some fun together.'

They'd been having a lot of fun right up until real life had barged in on them and burst their bubble. Up until the moment his love interest's protective big brother had come looking for her, they had been discovering their own little piece of paradise. Alone in that room, in each other's company, in each other's arms it had been easy to forget their lives outside that door and not consider the consequences of their actions. Such as protection. They hadn't discussed it and Joe had definitely been too carried away in the moment to think about it. Although his body had protested at Peter's interruption perhaps it hadn't been as ill-timed as he'd first thought.

A pregnancy would not have been a souvenir either of them would want to take away from this holiday romance. Emily was just getting her life back on track after her ex-husband's betrayal and her bravery today was proof of that. She didn't need to be tied to him for the rest of her days and vice versa. His personal issues would forever cloud any sort of long-term relationship and while this was still only a fling there was no reason to start trying to explain them. Unlike Emily, he wasn't ready to share them publicly.

'I thought I could trust you, man. You know what she's been through.'

'Yeah, and she needs this time away to try and forget it. I promise I won't do anything to hurt her.' He wouldn't be able to live with himself if he did. There'd be no trek long enough, or climb high enough to help him forget intentionally hurting either of them.

'You'd better not. I'd hate to have to hand back my halo

and take up arms again.' At least there was a hint of humour in the thinly veiled threat.

Joe held his hand up. 'Hey, I don't want to be the one responsible for sending you back to the dark side.'

'Then stay away from my sister.'

Okay, there wasn't a trace of a veil hiding that one. If only it was as easy as keeping his distance. Been there, done that, ended up rolling around on the floor with her.

'Sorry, bro, but I'm not going to do that. I don't want any bad blood between us but I like Emily a lot.' Joe waited for the explosions to start as he defiantly went against his friend's wishes. He only hoped Emily was as steadfast in continuing the relationship after this or else putting his friendship with Peter in jeopardy was all for nothing.

Instead of further threats of fisticuffs, Peter let out a sigh. The resigned sound of his disappointment was almost as devastating to Joe's equilibrium as the right hook he'd been expecting. Although he didn't want to examine his feelings for Emily too deeply for fear of what he'd discover, it spoke volumes that he was willing to risk upsetting the very guy he'd come here to help.

'I guess it's my fault for pushing you two together but I thought I could trust you not to take advantage of her.'

Another blow where it hurt the most.

'I would never do that. I respect her too much.'

'It didn't look that way to me.'

Joe's insides shrivelled up with shame. It would be easy to misinterpret what had been happening between him and Emily as something tawdry when it had evolved so naturally and beautifully. He regretted Peter walking in on them but not a second of the evening up until then.

'I'm sorry if you saw anything untoward but at the end of the day Emily's a grown woman who makes her own decisions.' There it was, the comment that could finally break their bromance. He was effectively telling the guy to butt out.

'That lack of judgement is the reason she ran out here in the first place.' Another sigh. 'I could use a cup of kava right about now, and a bucket of eye bleach. Your bare backside is not an image I want to go to sleep with tonight.'

Joe exhaled a nervous laugh. 'In that case, what do you say we forget it ever happened? I promise not to hurt your sister and keep my backside covered at all times.' It was the best compromise he could come to and mean it. Anything more than that and he knew he'd have difficulty keeping his word. He and Emily still had unfinished business.

'Hmm. I guess that'll have to do but the first sign of Joe-related tears from my little sister—'

'I know, I know, I should start swimming.'

'As long as we're clear.'

'Crystal.'

It wasn't anything Joe hadn't expected. All things considered, he'd got off lightly. Yasi Island really had mellowed Peter out. In another time and place he wouldn't have thought twice about knocking him out and Joe wouldn't have blamed him. He'd spent many a long night on training exercises talking about his family, shared all the big achievements in Emily's life with Joe as he'd read about them in cherished letters he'd received in Afghanistan. It was only natural tonight would seem like a betrayal and only time would let him prove otherwise.

As they reached the chief's house he was glad they'd kind of cleared the air. Whatever was ailing the patient inside was undoubtedly going to be difficult enough to manage, without the added stress of a duel over Emily's honour. He glanced back, checking for signs of her following, and could just about make out a bobbing flicker of light snaking through the village in the distance. Whatever the rest of the night had in store for him, he knew he would get through it better with her at his side.

CHAPTER NINE

EMILY KNEW JOE would have everything under control until she got there. At least as far as the medical emergency went. There were no obvious signs of a scuffle as she followed in their wake to the chief's house. She hadn't stumbled over any bodies so she'd take that as a sign he and Peter had either worked things out or chosen to ignore the humiliation they'd all just endured. It was going to take her longer to get over it.

She prayed Joe's quick actions had covered most of her blushes but it hadn't been enough to disguise what they'd been up to. Peter definitely would not approve, not because he was a prude, he was an ex-soldier after all, but because she'd chosen his best friend to get over her break-up. At the same time she realised Joe wasn't something she was willing to give up. Not yet. That time would come soon enough and she didn't want to miss out on anything he had to offer.

Tonight had only been a taster of what they could have together and not something she would easily forget when her body was still thrumming with sexual awareness. As long as she remembered this wasn't real, that they were never going to be part of each other's lives away from here, she shouldn't have to worry about anything other than enjoying the moment with Joe. Well, apart from her stepbrother walking in on them after passion had taken hold.

A shudder ripped through her. She was an adult, one who'd gone through an acrimonious split from her husband and deserved some fun and excitement in her life. That didn't mean one frowning look from her stepbrother wouldn't regress her back to that role of naughty kid sister, even when she hadn't done anything other than let loose for once. They were going to have to discuss what had happened, what was happening, between her and Joe so she could reassure him she knew what she was doing. Even when it seemed so far removed from her normal behaviour.

Joe and Peter already had proceedings under way when she caught up with them at either side of the patient's bedside.

'We thought he'd be more comfortable in my bed and we've stripped him down to try and bring down the fever.' Her stepbrother didn't waste any time on small talk, which suited her fine. They could discuss personal matters later in private, or not at all—either worked for her.

The small room was cramped with the chief and the three of them crowded inside, so she stood back, trying to remain invisible until she was needed. No such luck when Joe had anything to do with it.

'I need a thermometer if you have one in there.'

She rummaged around her bag and produced one while he stood with his hand out, waiting, as if he was the lead surgeon and she was the theatre nurse. It wasn't much of a stretch, she supposed, in this scenario where she was a spectator rather than the one taking readings.

'You've got a temperature of forty degrees, so we really need to get that down. I'll need plenty of water to keep him hydrated and we could use something to keep him sponged down. It would really help if we could clear as many people out of here as possible. Emily, I'm going to need your help to get this under control.' The crowd parted like the Red Sea to make a clear path between her and Joe, everyone watching for her reaction. Probably for different reasons.

'I'll get the water.' Peter's gaze flitted suspiciously between them as though they were trying to engineer another reason to be alone.

He shouldn't have worried. Emily needed time to process what had taken place tonight before they ended up back in the same scenario. It seemed neither of them were able to control themselves when left to their own devices and as yet she hadn't decided if that was detrimental to her well-being or not. Physically, there was no doubt they were compatible. It was the more *personal* aspects of getting involved that caused her concern. Her emotions were still in recovery and she didn't think they could cope with another mauling, no matter how unintentional.

Eventually Peter made a move towards the door, with the chief soon following behind.

Although it didn't make the room any less suffocating as she had to face Joe and try not to mention the incredible time they'd had together before fate had intervened.

'Nete is presenting with fever, along with muscle and joint pain. Did you bring some paracetamol?' He put her to shame with his thoughts being solely for his patient and not lingering back at their love shack. From here on they were merely medical colleagues working together to treat their patient. Everything beyond that could wait until their patient was back on track.

'Yes. That should help bring that temperature down too.' Important in preventing fits and further complications.

'Can you sit up for me?' He put a hand on the young

man's back and eased him up from the bed amid a lot of wincing.

Joe gestured for her to stand beside him. It was only then that she noticed the rash dotted across Nete's flushed skin, little islands of white in a sea of red.

'Have you been near any stagnant water recently?'

Emily's mind had instantly gone to all of those childhood illnesses mostly eradicated via the vaccination programme back home, but Joe obviously had different ideas about the source of the rash.

'I was down by the river a few days ago.'

Joe frowned, clearly disturbed by the information.

She knew herself that areas of stagnant water were a breeding ground for mosquitoes, airborne viruses and bad news.

'Could you get me the blood-pressure cuff, Emily?'

'I'm just going to wrap this around your arm,' she said to Nete. 'There will be a tightening sensation as we inflate the cuff but there's no need to panic. It's just how we test your blood pressure.' She knew the patient was too lethargic to really pay attention to what they were doing but it was important for her to have a role here and not fall back into the old pattern of feeling surplus to requirements. Joe had specifically asked her to assist him and this kind of emergency was exactly why she was here.

The lines on Joe's forehead grew deeper with the low reading she recorded. Although low blood pressure could be a sign of good health and fitness in someone of this age, coupled with the other symptoms it could be an indicator of heart or neurological disorders.

Joe loosened the cuff, squinting at the arm beneath as he did so and refastening it. 'I'm just going to do something called a tourniquet test. This means the cuff will tighten again for a few minutes.'

Emily watched in silence as he inflated it to the midpoint between the systolic and diastolic blood pressures, unease snaking through her body. She'd read up on tropical illnesses before venturing out here to practise and the tourniquet test was used to diagnose something far more serious than gastroenteritis. Dengue fever, also known as break-bone fever because of the associated joint pain. It was no wonder he was whimpering with pain even in his dazed state or that Joe was becoming increasingly concerned.

There was the threat of potentially fatal dengue haemorrhagic fever or dengue shock syndrome, neither of which they were equipped to treat. There was no intensive care unit in which to treat him if he needed it. Neither was there access to laboratory tests to confirm the initial diagnosis, which was why they would have to rely on this tourniquet test. With more than twenty petechial red spots from broken capillary blood vessels visible per square inch of skin, Joe's hunch was proved right.

There was no part of that diagnosis she found positive. Not only had she missed it, they were going to have a fight on their hands if his condition worsened.

'Okay, we'll let you rest again but you're going to have to sit up and make sure you drink plenty. Emily and I will go and see where Peter got to with that water.' Joe undid the cuff and tried to make him comfortable again before gesturing for Emily to join him outside.

'How did you know it was dengue?' It would probably have been well down her list of possibilities causing the patient so much discomfort and she could've wasted precious time in reaching the same diagnosis.

'I've seen it a few times on my travels. It's a nasty one. The rash and the joint pain are usually the main indicators, along with the more common symptoms.'

'What's the best way to approach this?' She wasn't

afraid to defer to him on this subject since it wasn't something she'd ever come across before.

'We need to keep an eye on him through the night in case his condition worsens. For now the paracetamol and tepid sponging should help control the fever at least, and if need be we can hook up an IV to make sure his fluid levels are balanced. We don't want to give any NSAIDs, such as ibuprofen or aspirin, in case they aggravate the risk of bleeding.'

Peter arrived back to meet them outside the room with the water and cloths. 'Bad news?'

Their faces must've expressed their concerns that a secondary infection could complicate matters beyond their capabilities with the limited medical supplies they had available.

'Dengue.' Joe shared their suspicions with Peter, then went back into the house to break it to the rest of the family, leaving her alone with her stepbrother and an awkward silence.

In the end Emily decided in the spirit of her new bolder persona she should be the one to broach the subject causing the tension. Except she didn't know how to appropriately rephrase, 'I know you're mad at me for getting jiggy with your mate but I literally fancy the pants off him.'

'I really like him. Joe, that is.' She went with inarticulate phrasing in the end.

Peter screwed his eyes tightly shut as though he was still trying to rid himself of the memory. 'I think I got that.'

'I mean, we didn't plan anything but we're, er, enjoying each other's company while we're here.' Her cheeks were burning as she tried to explain her outrageous behaviour to her religious sibling.

'As it was pointed out to me earlier, it's your life, Emily. But I would hate to see you get hurt. I've known Joe a long time. He's a good guy but he's not the commitment type. You've only just come out of a long-term relationship, your only relationship, and I don't want you to think he's the answer to being on your own. He'll be back on his travels in another couple of weeks.'

'So will I. You don't have to worry, I'm going into this with my eyes fully open. I know you're all loved up with Keresi at the minute, but the last thing I want is to be tied to another man.' However this progressed she was under no illusion that she was going home as part of a couple. The most this could ever be was a fling, a temporary arrangement, if that's what they both wanted.

'It's that obvious, huh?' It was refreshing to see her stepbrother take his turn at blushing. This woman clearly meant a lot to him. On the plus side, it took the onus off her and Joe.

'Well, not in the "found half-naked together" sense of obvious, but, yeah, I can tell. Is it serious?'

'We've been hanging out a lot and, yeah, I think I'm in deep.' His bashful smile said as much.

Emily gave him a playful punch on the arm, careful not to spill any of the water he was carrying. 'I'm so happy for you. For us.' She wanted him to understand they were both where they wanted to be in terms of relationships, or non-relationship in her case. The jury was still out on the official classification of her status.

'I haven't decided if I'll be leaving with you at the end of the month. I might stick around a while longer.'

'You do whatever feels right. I can always come back and visit when I need a bro-fix.' She smiled for his benefit, even though her heart broke a little more at the thought of losing him to Yasi permanently. Not that she would begrudge him this island paradise or a chance at happiness. She envied it.

'I haven't made any decision yet.'

'Something tells me you'll find it hard to leave.' She knew she would. If she had the choice between her lonely existence, bound by the rules of her position and the confinement of her office, or the freedom to help people out here with Joe by her side, she knew which one she'd take now.

'All I can do is take each day as it comes.'

'Is that the island motto or something? They should print that on T-shirts and sell them as souvenirs,' she said with a touch of bitterness. It was easier to do that when your days weren't limited to double digits.

He gave a hearty laugh, which did nothing to alleviate this particular case of the green-eyed monster. The clock was ticking on whatever this was with Joe, and she didn't have the luxury of deciding its fate. Peter didn't know how lucky he was. For her the dream would all be over too soon.

With the pressure of time weighing heavily on her mind, she thought of her patient, to whom it mattered most tonight. The next hours would be crucial in determining the severity of his illness and how effectively they'd be able to manage it.

'I should get back to work and take this water in before it reaches room temperature.'

'I'll give you a hand.'

True to his word, Peter helped her to get Nete upright and helped him drink the water, while she sponged him down. It wasn't long before Joe came back to join them and sent at least one temperature in the room soaring back up again.

'Isn't there a drug or something we can give him to counteract this?' Peter quizzed them, as he struggled to keep the lethargic patient upright.

'If only.' There was nothing she wanted more than to be able to give this boy a tablet and fix everything that ailed him. That was the kind of medicine she was used to—diagnosis, treatment, cure. Rare illnesses such as dengue weren't something she came across very often and when they did crop up the patients were invariably referred elsewhere. That wasn't an option out here. Even if they could get him transported to hospital, the journey alone could kill him. Seeing Nete in pain, following his progress right through, somehow made it real and personal. It was down to her and Joe to get him through this and out the other side.

Joe took another temperature reading and shook his head. 'There might be one thing we can try…'

As Emily took a peek at the thermometer she knew they needed to try something more than they were already doing. 'What is it?'

Joe exhaled a hard breath and it was a few heartbeats before he spoke as if he was debating whether or not his idea was even worth sharing. 'I mean, it's not scientifically proven or anything but when I was in India I saw them use the juice from papaya leaves to treat dengue.'

'Papaya leaves?' Although it wouldn't do any harm to try, Emily wasn't convinced that would really make much difference to his condition.

'I know it sounds ridiculous but I did do some follow up research into the properties of papaya leaves after seeing them used. Apparently they are packed with enzymes that are supposed to help clot the blood and normalise platelet count. It's worth a shot, right?' He was the only one offering a blink of hope, no matter how far away it appeared from the current reality of the situation.

'Definitely, but where do we get them and what do we do with them?' It was at times like this she missed the luxury of twenty-four-hour supermarkets and smoothie bars. She was too used to the convenience of modern life, and making simple requests like this without them seem impossible.

'I'm sure someone will know where to find them, then all we have to do is crush them.' Joe made it sound so simple when it scared Emily to put her faith in anything other than conventional medicine. That was probably the beauty of them working together and combining their so very different experiences.

'I know where we can find some. I'll go. I'm sure you can manage without me.' Peter gave a wry smile as he left on his mission. He clearly wasn't about to let go of her embarrassment any time soon but a nod and a wink was better than a frowny face and a half-battered Joe.

The patient gave a soft snore, oblivious to events unfolding all around him. They'd let him sleep through the pain until Joe concocted his marvellous medicine. In the meantime, Emily took the small battery-operated fan she kept in her bag and set it by the bed. Every little bit helped.

'Are things okay with you two, then?' She figured it was safe to ask now the initial awkwardness appeared to have passed.

'Yeah. We're good. You?'

She nodded. They'd known their actions would complicate all manner of things and yet that hadn't mattered at the time. It shouldn't matter now either since they'd addressed Peter's concerns. 'I can't say he's ecstatic about it but he knows where we're coming from. I think he's dodging Cupid's arrows himself at the minute.'

'I would say that little sucker struck his target long ago.' Joe's laugh reached across the bed to her and all the way down to curl her toes. She was already missing that carefree couple of hours they'd had. Who knew when they'd get to spend time together again? Or if it would ever be quite the same now they'd always be on their guard?

'Well, I hope he didn't give you too much of a hard time.'

'Nothing I couldn't handle,' he said, with the sexy smile of a man secure in his own skin. He could look after himself but Emily knew he would never have lifted a hand to do anything against his best friend except in defence. Even then, she suspected, he might've let Peter vent his anger unchecked if it made him feel better.

'There wasn't any blood spilled so I'd call that a win. I wouldn't want to be the cause of any unpleasantness between you.' She was fully aware of the special bond they had and, as far as she could see, the only real friend each of them had. It would be selfish of her to think a holiday fling should mean more to Joe than everything he'd gone through with Peter.

Joe carefully laid the cold cloth he was holding across Nete's forehead and walked around to the side of the bed where she was standing. There was definitely a shift in the atmosphere as he took her hand and turned her to face him, as if by entering her personal space he'd pushed out all the negative space around her and replaced it with crackling sexual energy.

'For the record, it would've been totally worth it.' His voice was a gravelly aphrodisiac, taking her right back to that moment before Peter had interrupted them. She'd been hovering on the brink of something amazing and she knew she wanted to go back there some time soon once they knew their patient was out of danger.

'I'm glad you think so.' Her mouth was suddenly dry and she had to moisten her lips with her tongue before she was able to speak. It hadn't been intended as a provocative action but she didn't miss the flare of desire in Joe's eyes as he watched her. They'd better get a move on with that miracle cure.

'I know so.' He dipped his head and left the ghost of a kiss on her lips; too quick to make a solid physical impact but with enough intention to stop her fretting that their time had already passed. There was still hope they could explore this chemistry if and when the opportunity arose again. Despite all the obstacles, Joe still wanted her and that was the best medicine in the world for her.

Joe hated it that they were pinning everything on this bowl of green mush on his say-so. Perhaps he should have kept it to himself and simply passed this off as an energy drink. That way the consequences of its failure wouldn't rest entirely on his shoulders. If this didn't work, the boy's condition was entirely down to the fates. Best-case scenario, he would recover on his own anyway. Worst-case scenario could lead to organ dysfunction, toxic shock and other life-threatening complications that required hospital intervention. Not two travelling doctors with little more than a first-aid kit.

He crushed the leaves with the wooden pestle and mortar he'd borrowed and ground away his fears before anyone could see them. As he'd watched the medicine men in India do, he squeezed the juice out into a bowl with his bare, clean hands. They didn't dilute the juice with water or add salt or sugar so neither did he, unwilling to take the chance of reducing its benefits.

'We need you to sit up and drink this.'

Peter and Emily took one arm each to help Nete sit up while Joe tilted the bowl to his lips for him to sip at. He hadn't tasted the juice himself but the sight of it and the patient's puckered mouth told him it didn't have the sweet, palatable taste of commercial medicines.

It had taken Peter a good couple of hours to source the papaya leaves for him, during which time he and Emily had managed to set aside their unresolved personal feelings for one another and focus on their patient's recovery. They'd seen a small decrease in his temperature as a result of the course of treatment provided already but not enough to sit back. The fever itself, he knew, could be biphasic, breaking and returning, and any sudden disappearance could be one of the warning signs of dengue haemorrhagic fever, the next critical level of the condition.

'When will we know if this is working?' Nete was understandably anxious for an instant cure for his pain but Joe didn't want to make any definite promises.

'You'll have to keep taking the juice at regular intervals through the night, I'm afraid.' He shot Emily a look of apology too since this was the first time she was hearing the news.

'We're all in for a long night by the sound of it.' Emily threw her hat in the ring to become part of the night watch alongside him.

Peter, on the other hand, already looked dead on his feet after his mad dash across the island, to retrieve the precious foliage. He'd done his part and keeping him here wouldn't serve any real practical purpose.

'I think you could use a few hours' sleep, mate. If you want to grab forty winks while you can, we'll give you a shout if we need your help.'

'I'll be fine,' Peter protested, blinking his eyes open wide.

'The last thing we need is to be another man down because you've overdone it. Now, take the advice of *two* doctors and get some sleep. You can take the next shift. Scoot.' Emily was the one to finally shoo him away so they could concentrate on the one patient they already had.

They'd do that better without the spectre of their indiscretion lingering in the room between them. Peter's reluctance to leave them alone again was proof enough that he hadn't got over it yet, even if they'd decided to leave it behind them until they had time and space to deal with it. Or carry on where they'd left off.

When it came to Emily all his common sense seemed to go out of the window and he could no longer predict his own actions from one minute to the next. Ordinarily he thrived on that level of excitement but tonight's events had shown him just how destructive that lapse in judgement could be. By continuing relations with Emily he was playing a dangerous game but he didn't think it was one he could quit any time soon.

'I don't know how you managed to keep control of an entire regiment. One pig-headed male is more than enough to deal with,' Emily huffed, as she won the battle of wills and common sense with her stepbrother.

To her it was a throwaway comment more about man's inability to admit personal weakness, something he knew a lot about. To him, any reference to his role in the military was a stark reminder of all the people he'd let down when they'd needed him most.

'I'm not sure I did.'

'There's no need for modesty. I'm sure you saved the lives of countless men on the front line and I know you pulled Peter out of a few tight spots.'

The patient was sleeping soundly now between them, dosed with papaya leaf juice and paracetamol and as cool as they could get him for now, so Joe stepped back from the bed for a little more space. He took a seat on the floor in the corner of the room and sipped at the cool water the chief had provided for them. Unfortunately, Emily followed him, apparently determined to carry on this conversation.

He'd probably played a part in saving lives in close-quarter combat. There were fleeting memories of bullet-ridden and shattered men he'd patched up and sent back in Chinooks to the base hospital, who he knew had later recovered from their injuries, but those faded against the vivid images of the last ambush he'd been caught up in.

He'd had to rely on the expertise of other medical personnel through that one when he'd *become* one of the casualties instead of being the one helping them.

'I did what I had to.' Mostly.

He took another sip of water, even the thought of the desert heat and that feeling of powerlessness making his mouth dry. Emily was oblivious to his discomfort, leaning forward, her head resting on her chin, listening intently as though he was telling her a bedtime story and not recounting the horrors of war.

'Do you miss it? I mean, I know Peter found it hard to adjust to civilian life again. I imagine it must be harder still if you were battling to save lives every day and suddenly no longer practising medicine. That must have been a huge departure for you.'

'It wasn't my choice.' The injustice of the situation forced its way to his lips before he could stop the words forming.

Emily cocked her head to one side, no doubt waiting for an explanation. He sighed, resigned to the fact he was going to have to reveal his biggest shame. Worse than that, he'd have to watch her reaction to it. Details of his hearing loss weren't something he often discussed. Generally he didn't stay in company long enough for it to become apparent. Asking people to repeat themselves, or missing snippets of conversation altogether, only became an issue if it was an ongoing problem. He didn't see the need to highlight his weakness and face more discrimination, decisions made on his behalf because of a perceived disability. The only reason he was considering telling her about it now was because she'd been brave enough to face her demons in his presence. Now it was his turn.

He took a deep breath.

'I had to take medical retirement after the IED that killed Batesy and Ste.' He debated whether or not to go as far as spilling his guts over the guilt he felt over the incident but decided against it. No one would ever understand how much his failing had affected him, still affected him, and he didn't expect them to. That was his own personal wallowing pool.

When Emily didn't launch into her usual line of questioning, which he'd expected to draw the information out gradually, he was forced to elaborate.

'The explosion damaged my hearing and the army decided they didn't want to take the chance of having a partially deaf soldier on the front line who couldn't hear the enemy coming.' The irony was that it was the stealth of the insurgents that had done the damage in the first place.

'Couldn't you have continued your medical expertise in one of the hospitals or in some sort of training capacity?'

There had been no gasp of shock as he broke the news. Although he wasn't looking for sympathy, he had expected some sort of emotional reaction. Here he was, spilling a secret so easily to her that usually only came out when circumstances forced it from him, and she was treating it as a minor ailment that could've been remedied with some paperwork shuffling. She should've understood how great the loss of his career had been when she was so tied to her own. If it wasn't for her own medical expertise keeping her afloat in the aftermath of her marriage she might have felt just as lost as he had when he'd first left the army.

'I was a soldier as well as a medic. I belonged in the field, not cooped up in some *safe* place while the rest of my colleagues were risking their lives. That blast stole my career from me and left me half the man I used to be.' There, he'd spelled it out to her in case she was missing the bit about him essentially being worthless to the army.

'It may have felt like that at the time but you're so much

more than the army. You've proved that with the work you've done here, and everywhere else on your travels.'

Joe wasn't sure if he imagined her flinching at the picture he'd painted since she spoke so coolly. Too coolly. Too precisely. Now he thought about it, he hadn't once had to ask her to repeat herself or speak up since they'd first met. She always spoke clearly, facing him, so he could read her lips, even if he couldn't hear her every word.

'You already knew.' The realisation hit him hard. All this time he'd been trying to impress her and she'd probably been aware of his inadequacy all along.

'Sorry?'

'Peter told you why I had to leave the army?'

The blush gave her away even before she confirmed his hunch. 'Only because I thought you were being rude by ignoring me.'

'I get that a lot.' He managed a half-smile at the thought of how riled she must've been at him for Peter to have told her. It was some consolation he hadn't simply been the subject of gossip between them but telling Emily was a big deal for him. It should have been his decision, his privilege to tell her.

'I think that makes us even. My secret for yours.' Emily nudged him, trying to make light of the moment.

It would be easy for him to lose his rag and tell her it was none of her business but she wasn't to blame for his inability to deal with this. No one was, not even Peter. He couldn't hide away from his hearing issue for ever and if he took a leaf out of her book he'd front it out and people would simply have to accept it. The strength of her courage became even more apparent when he thought of shining a spotlight on his insecurity for the whole world to see. Still, he'd share details of his deafness before he'd let anyone in on the events of that fateful day and his responsibility for it.

'How about a pact never to mention either?'

'Done.'

'And in answer to your original question, yes, I do miss it. Not the heat or the injuries my friends suffered, but the excitement and that sense of belonging. I had a role, a reason to be.' He shut his mouth before he said anything more. It wasn't in his nature to take a dip in self-pity, and especially not with spectators. Coming across as a sad sack certainly wasn't going to improve his chances of finishing what he'd started with Emily tonight. He was supposed to be the fun, uncomplicated side of this partnership. A traumatised ex-vet who needed sex to justify his existence probably wouldn't seem as attractive.

'You have a role out here. You're needed here. But I guess that's why you don't stick around. It never gets dull for you if you're always moving from one place to another.' Emily hugged her knees against her chest as she psychoanalysed him. Joe guessed she found that harder to understand than him hiding his disability when stability and security seemed to be what she craved most in her life. Things she would never find with him.

'Exactly. New places, new people get the adrenaline pumping for me.' The closest he came to that without leaving the island was when he and Emily were alone together. That was when he felt most alive, most validated as a person.

Once she left Yasi there would be absolutely no reason for him to stick around.

CHAPTER TEN

'MORNING.' EMILY YAWNED a greeting to Peter and Miriama as she passed them in the hallway. She and Joe had managed to grab a few hours' sleep on a couple of makeshift mattresses close by when they'd volunteered to take over the early morning shift. She thought all was well since she'd been left to wake up in her own time, until she saw that Joe had already vacated his bed.

'Morning.' Peter handed her some lemon tea, its bitter zing guaranteed to wake her up.

She cradled the cup in her hands, letting the comforting warmth spread through her weary body before she took a sip. 'How is Nete?'

'He's a bit brighter today. Joe's with him if you want a professional assessment.'

She trusted Peter's word but she did want to see for herself. An early morning Joe fix might just set her up for the day too.

'Hey,' she said when she saw Joe, thinking how unfair it was that he still looked devastatingly handsome on so little sleep. No doubt she had the world's worst bed hair and panda eyes, while his crumpled clothes and morning stubble simply elevated his hunk status.

'Hi, sleepyhead.' He had the bright eyes and cheerful

demeanour of someone who'd been awake for a while, or had somehow got his hands on a shot of *actual* caffeine.

Either way, she would have preferred to have been included than not. 'You should have woken me.'

'You were sleeping so soundly I hated to disturb you. Besides, you probably wouldn't have heard me above your snoring.' He shared the joke with their patient, who was now sitting up unassisted and laughing at her expense.

'I do not snore!' At least, she didn't think she did, unless a year of sleeping alone had somehow caused it to manifest. She was sure Greg would've told her if it had ever been a problem. He'd never been shy about pointing out her faults and not in such a jokey fashion either. In fact, she could see now that he'd been downright cruel at times, playing on her insecurities until she'd hated herself for not being the woman he'd obviously wanted.

At least now she was beginning to see she wasn't the only one who'd failed at that relationship. If Greg had accepted her as unconditionally as Joe seemed to, there would never have been a need to constantly belittle her. In hindsight that was probably what had made her cling to stability as much as she had. She'd needed something to make her feel safe and secure, with her husband constantly undermining her. Now that she'd moved on, found herself at peace with who she was, she didn't intend to return to that dark, uncertain place.

'I'm only messing with you. You needed the rest. I'm used to getting by on very little sleep.'

She faked a smile as he reminded her of their contrasting lifestyles. He was always going to be the drifter, content to take life one day at a time, when all she wanted was her own bed and job security. If she was realistic they'd probably only made a connection because they'd been thrown together on this tiny island and she didn't want to be with another man for all the wrong reasons.

'So, how are we getting on?' She glanced over the readings Peter had jotted down during the night, keeping track of his progress.

'Fever's broken, fluid intake is steady, as is urine output, and he's hungry, which is always a good sign.' Relief was etched all over Joe's smiling face, even though he hadn't once given in to panic during their stint last night.

'I'm so glad to hear that.' At times it had been touch-and-go whether or not they'd get to this apparent recovery phase. They'd sweated right along with the patient through every painful stage of the illness. Not that it was over yet, but Joe was right, the outcome was looking more favourable now than it had done at certain low points of the night. It had been a long shift and she had a new-found respect for hospital workers for whom the long hours and clean-up were simply part of the job. All worth it, though, if it meant the worst had passed.

'I think it's safe for us to nip home and get freshened up, if Peter and Miriama don't mind taking over here a bit longer?' Joe was able to put his question directly to the other volunteers as they entered the room on cue.

'No problem at all,' Miriama assured them both.

Emily would never dream of taking advantage but even a bucket of cold water seemed like a luxury right now to someone in last night's clothes who'd spent most of the last twelve hours mopping fevered brows and vomit.

'Er...the chief might have other ideas for you.'

Peter interrupted her immediate plans with a worrying comment. If there was some sort of ceremony to celebrate renewed health, Emily hoped she could still grab five minutes' privacy for a wash and change of clothes.

'We won't be long. Tell him we'll be back in our rightful places in no time at all.' Joe added his support to her cause, clearly with the same need to feel human again. They couldn't possibly be taken seriously as medical professionals dressed in wrinkled date-night clothes as if they'd just stumbled in from a club.

'Yeah, yeah, you can still go and get changed. I mean he has plans for the rest of your day. He wants to throw a beach picnic in your honour for saving his son.'

'That sounds lovely.'

'There's really no need. Besides, we're not completely out of the woods yet.' Joe talked over her acceptance with some uncharacteristic reluctance to take part on one of the spontaneous gatherings.

Emily pouted as the menfolk battled to plan her day for her. 'I haven't seen the beach since the day I arrived. You're the one who's always telling me to chill, take time out for me and stop stressing about deserting my post. Or is that only when it suits you?'

This was coming close to their first real argument, but while she was bracing herself for a showdown, Joe clenched his jaw and bit back whatever retort was on his tongue.

'He really wants to show you his gratitude and we can hold the fort for you here until you get back. You both need the break.' Peter was so insistent it would be a shame to send him back to the chief with bad news.

'We'd love to, wouldn't we, Joe?' She pushed her luck that tiny bit further. Once he had time to think about it he'd see some fresh air, a paddle in the sea and a picnic lunch might be the best medicine to revitalise two weary medics.

Neither his scowl nor his grunt were in keeping with that theory but he didn't object verbally and she took that as an uneasy acceptance. A complete role reversal from their usual power play. This time she was the one pushing him to try something different. Emily understood his concerns but the others were well versed in the treatment to give in their absence. Bar chartering a private plane to get their patient to a hospital, there was little more any of them could do if his condition worsened. The next time this illness struck the island it was entirely possible Miriama would be the only person here to treat it anyway. At least, that's how Emily justified this time out to herself.

It wasn't long before she and Joe were heading back to get ready for their lunch date, regardless of his reluctance to join the 'keep calm and carry on' party.

'You shouldn't have done that.'

'Why not? I think we earned a break. Anyway, aren't you the one always reminding me how much I'll offend people by not participating in these things? It's lunch, not a mutiny. I'm still coming back to resume my doctor duties once I've been fed. It might not be up to the culinary standards of your beans on toast feast but I'm hungry, sleep-deprived and generally in need of some me time. That might sound selfish but I think a less grouchy me will benefit everyone in the long run. We'll be back before you know it.'

She could see why he was so concerned about leaving their patient but she genuinely believed Nete was over the worst of it and they wouldn't be gone for too long. It was never going to be a continuation of their ruined date with so many others in attendance but it would do them good to get out of there for a while.

'That won't be as soon as you think.'

'What makes you say that?'

'Their idea of a beach picnic is on another island. It's a beautiful place but not very practical for getting back to a patient in the event of an emergency.'

'Why on earth didn't you tell me?' She wanted to scream at him for standing back while she'd blathered on about what *she* needed. If she'd known it would come at the possible cost of their patient's welfare she never would've pursued this.

He shrugged, increasing the chances of her giving those shoulders a shake herself. 'You didn't give me much of a chance. You seemed so determined to accept and I didn't want to worry the others unnecessarily.'

But it was apparently okay to make her more anxious by keeping the details to himself until it was too late to do anything. She ground her teeth, stifling her exasperation.

'Now what do we do?' She'd landed them in a tricky situation, caught between offending the chief and potentially jeopardising his son's health.

'Now we go and put on our beach clothes and graciously accept our host's invitation. We'll leave instructions for the treatment we would've carried out ourselves and keep our fingers crossed this works out.' His smile didn't travel any further than his lips and Emily knew it was only to placate her.

She'd messed up but something told her Joe would be the one to accept responsibility should the worst happen.

So much for acting spontaneously. It never ended well for her.

CHAPTER ELEVEN

AFTER HER LONGED-FOR freshen-up, Emily decided to go with the outfit she'd worn when she'd first arrived on the island. The maxi-dress wasn't any more practical than the last time but it was comfortable and put her back in holiday mode. The deed was done, they were leaving the island, so she may as well enjoy it.

She met up with Joe where they'd had that initial encounter at the water's edge, although there were a few more island greeters this time. He was wearing the same outfit as he had that day too, which she put down to their strong connection—or karma. Or the distinct lack of wardrobe choices available to them on the island.

At least he was smiling properly this time as he walked towards her. 'I've left the locum doctors with enough papaya leaves to paper the room with and a promise we'll be back before nightfall.'

'I'm sure everything will be fine.' She was trying to convince herself since it was too late to undo her mistake without causing panic.

They joined the small band of locals weighed down with armfuls of food for their day out. It seemed an age since she'd landed here with no knowledge of what she'd been getting herself into. Only a few days later she had friends who wanted to throw her a celebratory lunch, and a man who seemed to like her. If they ever found themselves alone again they might actually get to explore what that meant.

'You look beautiful, by the way,' he said, and pressed a kiss to her cheek, drawing a few giggles from the kids in the assembled crowd.

'I'm actually quite excited about this.' She meant about their island hopping but it worked for Joe kisses too. No matter how chaste, or not, the second his lips touched her she was on fire with desire for him. Sooner or later she was going to have to let it burn itself out or extinguish the flames altogether. In the end there would be nothing but ashes left anyway and a memory of what could have been.

'So are they.' He nodded in the direction of their happy travelling companions who'd come together in their honour. Those who could afford to take some time out of their busy day, at least. She and Joe really were very privileged to have such generosity bestowed on them when resources were so limited out here. That kind of respect and appreciation meant more to her than monetary bonuses or finishing work on time every night. There was a definite attraction to the laid-back lifestyle out here that wasn't just about her co-worker.

'Where is this place we're going to?' Her adventurous spirit hadn't completely run away with her. On seeing their mode of transport, a couple of dinghies that looked as though they'd been washed ashore during the last hurricane, she was suddenly keen to remain within swimming distance of Yasi. They definitely weren't in any condition to go out on the open sea but the chief was beaming with so much pride as he ushered them on board he could've been giving them a tour of the islands on his private yacht.

'Not too far. There's a small uninhabited island just across the bay.'

'A *real* desert island?' That was something she'd only

seen in the movies, usually involving starving cast-
aways driven mad by heatstroke and loneliness. It wasn't
a thought she relished on her own but with food and company, and the means to leave again, she knew it could
turn out to be one of the highlights of her trip. Once she
stopped imagining falling overboard and being stranded
with nothing to eat but coconuts, she was able to focus
on the merits of such a setting. Sand, sea and a sexy side-
kick were the makings of a very different kind of film.

They all piled into the two boats, with the majority
of the islanders in one dinghy, and Emily, Joe, the chief
and the food in the other. This was obviously a treat for
everyone and not something they did on a whim, given
the level of excitement as the engine spluttered into life.
It seemed this was the Yasi equivalent of first class and
she should feel honoured, not clutching the side of the
boat and praying.

'Stop worrying.' Joe prised her fingers loose and set
her hand back in her lap, with his resting on top.

She closed her eyes and did her best not to imagine a
watery grave as he gave her hand a reassuring squeeze,
and she knew he'd keep her safe no matter what. The wind
whipped through her hair, blowing away her residual fears
as they skimmed the waves towards sanctuary. It was easy
to imagine this was all an illusion created by her lack of
sleep but the sea spray splashed her face, reminding her
this *was* real even when it seemed too fantastic to be true.
Nonetheless, when they cut the engine and came ashore,
she had to restrain herself from jumping overboard and
kissing the sandy ground. She took off her sandals as Joe
helped her off the boat so her footprints were the first to
mark the untouched beach.

Not for the first time she wished she'd brought a camera to document her travels. At the time of leaving England she'd been so eager to distance herself from reality

she'd left all traces of the modern world behind her, including her phone. There was something so symbolic about that single track of footprints in the sand, marking her bold journey into the unknown, she'd never forget it.

When she reached a line of trees and looked back to see Joe making his way across the beach, leaving a second set of prints alongside hers, it didn't lessen the powerful image. He'd been very much a part of this adventure with her, coaxing this slightly braver Emily to explore beautiful new vistas. She didn't want to leave any of it behind in case she forgot it, or vice versa. Everything here had made such an impact on her for the better and she hoped she'd made some sort of lasting impression on Yasi, on Joe. It didn't seem fair to be falling so heavily for someone if she turned out to be nothing more than a side note in his travel journal.

She knew that's what was happening when she was so conflicted about what she wanted from this trip and from him. If he hadn't already claimed a piece of her heart she wouldn't be overanalysing every move about how it would affect her and simply go with her natural urges. It almost didn't matter if they took that next step together when the damage had already been done. He'd breached her defences and left her vulnerable.

'It's beautiful here.' She tried to keep upbeat even though the shock of her discovery was enough to bring her to tears. The sky might be bluer than she thought naturally possible, the white sand warm under her feet, but she was still a fool when it came to men.

Joe had warned her off against getting into anything she couldn't handle but she'd convinced herself she was tough enough to deal with whatever happened. Now, after little more than a few snatched kisses, she knew her heart had lied to her. It hadn't been broken beyond all repair

after Greg, or why else would it ache so much for another man?

'I've been here a few times. It's a good spot to unwind.
Mind you, there's work to be done if we're going to eat
any time soon.' He pointed down at the rest of the islanders coming ashore in single file, carrying the food supplies, like an army of ants.

'I'm so sorry. I was so pleased to get here I didn't even
think about helping to unload the boats.' She must seem
so shallow and privileged to everyone else, used to muck-
ing in and doing their bit as part of the community. She'd
been living alone too long, concerned with nothing but
her own survival until now.

'It's okay. Everyone is assigned jobs to do. Ours is to
collect palm leaves.'

'Palm leaves? That's not lunch, is it?'

His laughter calmed her new food fears before they
fully formed. 'No. They're used for weaving into plates for
the food and as a makeshift picnic table. It means there's
no litter left behind when we're finished here.'

They carried out their new duties in silence, with Joe
cutting the leaves while she gathered them. She should
have known this would be more than the tartan rug and
plastic accessories she was used to in a basket. Then
again, lunch here was bound to be more than a soggy
sandwich and a packet of crisps. Even a simple picnic
turned into something exotic and exciting when it was
on one of these islands.

Never more so than when she saw how they were preparing the food. The *lovo*, as Joe explained to her, was an
oven built in the sand. Emily watched with fascination as
the men set a fire in the small pit and stacked rocks on
top until they were hot enough to cook the food on. Banana leaves were then placed on top as insulation to keep
the stones hot and moisture in the food while it cooked.

Emily sat with several of the women and children plait-
ing the palm fronds into primitive mats for the food and
Joe waded out into the water with the others for a spot of
net fishing. Part of her wished he was still wearing the
translucent white shirt from yesterday as his wet clothes
clung to him so she could have her very own Mr Darcy
moment. At least she had first-hand experience of every
solid inch of that torso to enable her imagination to by-
pass that dark perv-proof fabric. She fanned herself with
one of the long palm fronds as he strode from the sea,
water sluicing from his body as if he'd just walked out of
a dream. An erotic fantasy she'd take back to keep her
warm at night in her luxurious, but empty, bed.

'You'll be feasting today,' he promised her as they
brought their catch in. Soldier, medic, lumberjack,
fisherman—there seemed no end to his talents, or else
he never grew tired of acquiring them.

She supposed she'd managed to add mat weaver and
painter to her CV over the course of a couple of days
too. That was the thing about the island, a person never
seemed to be pigeonholed into one area of their life. It was
all about working together and sharing jobs and skills to
make sure the traditions never died out. One more thing
she would miss when she returned home. Little wonder
Joe couldn't see himself tied to a desk somewhere, shuffling paperwork, after trying his hand at so many new
experiences. She wasn't looking forward to it herself after
roaming free in the big wide world beyond her office
walls.

It took a couple of hours for the food to cook, during
which time she managed to cobble together a couple of
flat mats to keep their lunch sand-proof. She was starting
to see why the time frame for this meal had been such an
issue for Joe. It wasn't the forty-five-minute lunch break
she'd been expecting either, but it was worth it when the

banana leaves were lifted off to reveal the feast Joe had promised her.

As well as the *dalo* and cassava root vegetables she'd become accustomed to, today saw the addition of fresh fish and crab. It tasted all the better knowing Joe had provided it for her.

'At least I know I won't starve if we get shipwrecked here,' she said, scooping up another piece of crab meat with her fingers.

'I might not be perfect but I'll always make sure you're looked after.' He grinned and helped himself to another chunk of fish, oblivious to the thrill he'd given her with a few simple words.

A whoosh of something powerful shot through her veins, immediately revitalising her previously weary body. It was only a figure of speech but deep down she knew that promise was true. Joe was the only man other than her stepbrother she could trust not to hurt her. Her soft heart was trying to convince her she should be with him even if a few days together was all that was on offer. There was a chance she'd regret missing out on that time more than walking away from him at the end of this trip.

It didn't take long to clear away the evidence of their beach invasion and, lovely though it was, she was getting kind of antsy to return to Yasi. Once they'd checked in on their patient and made sure there was no medical emergency, she and Joe might actually get some privacy. If it took barricading the clinic door with the furniture she was willing to do it if it meant getting to explore the next level with him. Although she wasn't sure if that would make it better or worse when the time came to leave.

She and Joe made their way to the boat they'd arrived in, only to find the chief barring their way. 'I want to thank you for helping my son.'

'You already did that. This was lovely.' Every future

picnic was going to be held up to this standard. A blanket on wet grass with a basket full of cold cuts simply wasn't going to cut it any more when it would be up against an afternoon on a desert island with present company.

They tried again to step on board but the chief side-stepped in front of them again. 'We want to give you a gift. Some time alone. You can keep the boat until you're ready to return to Yasi. There is enough room in this one for all of us.'

'That's really not necessary—'

'We couldn't ask you to do that—'

They stumbled over each other's words in their hurry to get back on the boat. It was a lovely gesture that would've been very welcome in other circumstances but this gift of time didn't stop the clock elsewhere.

'It's very, very kind of you but we must see to your son.' Her heart was in her throat as she dared to refuse his generosity but she knew how anxious Joe had been about coming out here in the first place. She didn't want to prolong his agony, or have him more ticked off at her if she could help it. Their fragile relationship would splinter completely if it became the reason a patient had suffered.

The chief held his hand up. 'I insist.'

His authority dictated they comply or run the risk of upsetting the entire tribe by declining this huge privilege bestowed on them. She was going to leave the next move up to Joe since he knew them better than she did and she didn't want to be the one to make the final call.

The rest of the group were watching them anxiously and he could see Emily's silent plea for help in her wide eyes. As doctors they both wanted to do what was best for their patient but as a seasoned traveller he understood the importance of maintaining good relations with his hosts. To his knowledge, he, Peter and Emily had been the first

Westerners to ever set foot on this island owned by the Yasi-based tribe. It was a greater honour still for them to be offered use of their only transport for his and Emily's enjoyment. They were a conservative race when it came to personal relationships, especially outside marriage, but they were clearly giving them some space to be together without any interference, something he would've grabbed with both hands last night.

Now, going against everything he'd worked so hard to avoid, he was making decisions that could affect so many people. It was going to be up to him to get Emily back to Yasi in one piece, without upsetting anyone and making sure it was done in a timely fashion to prevent any further medical emergencies. He took a deep breath and girded himself for the challenge.

'We'll make sure we're back before sunset.'

He could already feel Emily's gaze burning into the back of his head so he did what any man would do and pretended not to notice. She was polite enough to wait until company was out of earshot before saying anything.

'I hope you know how to get us home. I'm putting all my faith in you,' she said, without taking her eyes off the dinghy sailing away, now full to capacity.

Dread settled in the pit of his stomach. That's what he was afraid of. It was one thing puttering out here on his own but quite another when he was responsible for Emily too. One could never plan for any unexpected catastrophes but that didn't mean you weren't left carrying the resulting guilt for the rest of your life. He was becoming too emotionally attached to these people being continually left in his charge and soon he was going to have to think about moving on.

If things weren't so complicated he would've used this time to his advantage to seduce Emily. The setting, if not the current mood, was the ideal place for them to finally consummate this attraction. Unfortunately, sex wasn't the only thing on his mind. It was having to wrestle with the dangers of the open water and the potential consequences of their absence on Yasi for prominence. For now they'd simply have to wait this out until an acceptable amount of time had passed to pacify their friends.

'Don't worry, I've done this before.' Although it was usually out of a necessity to have some space to himself rather than with enforced company.

'Oh. You mean you and the chief have some sort of understanding where he'll help you kidnap unsuspecting female tourists so you can hold them hostage here until you get your wicked way with them?' Emily folded her arms across her chest as she mocked him, stretching the light fabric of her dress taut across her bust and really not helping to take Joe's mind off the idea of seduction.

'Yeah. You got a problem with that?' They exchanged cheesy grins as their sense of humour thankfully took over from that initial urge to panic.

Emily laughed and shook her head. 'Nope. Except maybe next time you could give me some warning.'

'You're right. The timing was a little off on this one. In future I'll make sure we're better organised.' His mind flitted towards a day here together with no worries dragging them back to civilisation. They certainly wouldn't be standing here, fully dressed, counting the minutes until they could leave.

The sound of the waves lapping at their feet punctuated the sudden silence between them as what-might-have-beens stole away any further chat. It would be selfish of them to act on impulse now and get lost in each other. One taste of paradise and he knew he'd never want to leave.

With one quick movement he stripped off his shirt and his shorts to wade out into the water in nothing but his boxers. He needed to cool off.

'What are you doing?'

'Going for a swim. Come on in. The water's lovely.' He lay on his back, making small circles with his hands in the sea to keep him afloat, tempted to let the gentle current carry him away.

Emily dipped a toe in the water and stepped back again. 'Are there sharks in there?'

'I haven't seen any but they're not likely to come this close to the shore anyway.' He flicked his fingers, soaking her with spray.

She walked forward until the sea was swirling around her feet and lifting the hem of her dress. Joe held his breath as she revealed every sensual curve of her figure. It barely mattered she was wearing a pretty pink bikini beneath, she may as well have been naked the way his body was responding. She tossed the dress onto the sand and slowly waded out towards him.

Joe spluttered as water covered his face and filled his nostrils. He gulped a mouthful as he struggled to stand upright. He'd been so engrossed in the sight of her stripping off he'd forgotten he needed to work to stay afloat.

'You okay?'

He could hear the flicker of amusement in her voice even though he couldn't see her clearly as he scrubbed the water from his eyes. 'Sure. I think I just forgot to breathe there for a second.'

'How come?' Emily was a little breathy, treading water deeper out into the sea.

Joe swam out to meet her, gravitating towards her like she was his life raft in raging stormy seas. They faced each other, only their heads bobbing on the surface of the water, and he knew he couldn't lie. Either to her or himself.

'Because you're so beautiful.'

Emily immediately cast her eyes down, reluctant to

accept the truth of his compliment. If she wasn't going to listen to him then he was simply going to have to show her. He waded closer and captured her mouth with his, the salty and sweet taste of her lips a feast for his senses.

She wound her arms around his neck and he was happy to anchor her legs around his waist and take her weight. In fact, with her body pressed tightly to his, if they sank to the bottom of the sea and drowned he'd die happy. Denying themselves any longer when everyone already assumed they were together seemed futile, and by giving in to his urges he was finally able to breathe again. It seemed as though he'd been holding his breath since last night, waiting for permission to exhale, and Emily had granted him that the second she'd kissed him back.

There was a flash of light and it took a while for him to figure out it was coming from above and wasn't fireworks going off in his head. He opened his eyes to see clouds rolling in, the sky now a palette of murky greys and purples. A rumble sounded in the distance, just after a charge of electricity that seemed to reach up to the heavens.

'We need to get back to the beach and find shelter.'

'Hmm?' Emily was still nuzzling into him, oblivious to the danger around them, which was either a sign of how far she'd come or how great a kisser he was to make her overcome her natural worry state.

'There's. A. Storm. Coming.' It was difficult to get the sentence out when she insisted on kissing him between words and scrambling his brain. In the end he simply carried her ashore, still clinging to him like a limpet on the rocks. Not that he was complaining. It simply made it harder for him to care what was going on out there too.

He laid her down on the sand but she refused to release her hold, bringing him down with her. Making love to Emily here, with the waves drifting in and out between their naked bodies, was the stuff of fantasies but tropical storms came in hard and fast. That wasn't how he wanted their first sexual encounter to go just because they were in a race against the elements.

Another roar of thunder reverberated around them then the rain came down in sheets and poured cold water on their ardour. Emily shrieked and jumped to her feet.

'I did try to tell you,' he said, rolling onto his back to let the rain cool his fevered skin.

'What will we do?' Emily was already back in panic mode, grabbing up her clothes and looking to him for answers.

Joe donned his shorts and T-shirt with more urgency as the gap between the flashes of light and crashes of thunder became ever smaller. The storm was coming closer... the rain was reaching saturation point. If they didn't get struck by lightning first, their cold, wet clothes sticking to their bodies might lead to pneumonia. They needed to get somewhere that would shelter them from the elements and keep them safe and dry.

'I know somewhere.' He grabbed her hand and made a dash for higher ground. There was a recess cut into the rocks that he knew from experience would provide everything they needed until this storm passed. His secret until now.

They clambered up the boulders in the rain and Joe kept hold of Emily's hand until they made it to the rocky hidey-hole in case she slipped in her no-longer-practical sandals. It was dark inside but at least it was dry.

Emily was watching the storm from the entrance, her shoulders shaking from the cold.

'I'll start a fire to get us warmed up.' He wasn't as eager to have a ringside seat for the fireworks. Loud noises and bright lights weren't as attractive to him as they once might have been.

'How do you propose to do that?' Apparently man creating fire was more interesting than nature's fury as she turned her attention back to him.

'I could sit here half the night trying to get a spark from rubbing a couple of pieces of wood together, or we could just use these.' He was almost sorry to disappoint her with the kindling and box of matches he'd left after his last visit here instead of showing off his caveman skills. Modern fire-making methods were quicker but they weren't as manly as starting one from little more than sticks and friction.

'Wait, is this your *actual* man cave?' She said it as though it was something he should be ashamed of but this place had been his salvation at times, not merely some whimsical notion of reliving his youth.

'Sometimes a guy needs a little time out.' He shrugged it off. It was difficult to explain his need for time out now and again, away from even the small population of Yasi.

This retreat enabled him to maintain a physical and emotional distance when he was in danger of getting too close to the people he was working alongside. By bringing Emily here with him, he'd totally screwed with that idea. Now there was nothing keeping his heart out of matters. He was past the point of no return and the damage was done. There was no way he was going to walk away from this without collecting a new battle scar.

He hadn't even told Peter, his oldest friend, about this place. Peter, who, up until a few days ago, had been the closest person in his life, the only one keeping him out here. Somehow Emily had crept in and hijacked his affection. Why else would he be holed up here with her instead of doing his job back on Yasi?

He got to work setting the fire and Emily came to kneel beside him. 'You know, if this trip has taught me anything it's that it's more fun being around people than sitting moping on your own.'

'I spend plenty of time in company, have made acquaintances all around the world. I'm simply happier in my own company.' That wasn't necessarily true. *Safer* was the word he'd been searching for but he didn't want to get into that with Emily and have to explain why he didn't get involved with people. That meant sharing the most painful part of his life with her and publicly owning the part he'd played in the deaths of his friends. Something he'd never done with anyone.

'Would you prefer it if I left you alone?' Emily made a half-hearted attempt to leave but they both knew she wasn't going anywhere. Neither of them were until this storm had passed and it was safe for them to take the boat out again. Matters outside this cave were completely beyond their control.

'No.' He stood up to block her exit. 'I want you here with me.'

He meant it in every sense. He wanted her company, to share this space, and most of all to help him forget everything going on in the outside world. This was their time together when they were free to relax and be themselves, without any outside influence bursting their bubble.

Emily shivered as he reached for her.

'You know, it's going to take a while for this place to heat up. We should really get out of these wet clothes.'

He slipped one strap of Emily's dress over her shoulder, then the other, and watched the garment pool at her feet. She stood proudly before him, making no move to cover the rest of her body from view. In fact, she was already reaching up to undo her bikini top.

'I've heard the best way to fight hypothermia is to share body heat.'

'I've heard that theory.' He peeled off his T-shirt, eager to put it to the test.

Emily slowly and silently removed the last of her

clothes and time stood still for Joe. She was a goddess with a body worthy of being immortalised in marble to epitomise the beauty of woman. Her soft curves and perfect proportions deserved love sonnets written in her honour but he wasn't a sculptor or a poet. All he had to offer her was himself. So he unwrapped her gift as quickly as he could.

There was something very primitive about standing in a cave with a naked woman and his body responded accordingly. Thankfully his brain was still capable of making some of his decisions. If this was to be the only private time they were to have together, he wanted it to be truly memorable for both of them. They needed more than a frantic coupling on a cold floor.

He reached out to brush her wet hair from her shoulders and felt her tremble beneath his fingers.

'Are you still cold?' The blood pounding through his body had warmed him from the inside out so he'd assumed the same was true for her. He was relieved when she shook her head or else he really would have to start trying to get heat back into her body.

'Nervous.'

Her answer was full of her characteristic honesty. It didn't take a genius to work out he was probably the first man she'd done this with since her husband. Joe ignored all the warning signs flashing in his head about what that meant and accepted it as his privilege, not his downfall.

'There's no need. I won't do anything to hurt you.' All he wanted to do was please her, love her, make her feel as special as she deserved. He was going to be the one hurting when this fantasy ended. Emily would go home and probably find a new love, whereas he knew he'd never be this open again. She'd stolen a piece of his heart he'd never intended to give to anyone and would never, ever get it back.

It was his turn to tremble at the enormity of the revelation. They didn't have a future together when she couldn't rely on him to keep her safe when she needed him most. He would only let her down and he couldn't bear to disappoint her or, worse, face the agony of losing her because of his actions. He was in love with Emily but he couldn't tell her, couldn't do anything about it other than show her.

CHAPTER TWELVE

THERE WAS SOMETHING different about kissing a woman he was in love with. Something familiar, as if he'd found a missing part of himself, yet with an element of danger attached. He was used to living life on the edge but for once he was actually afraid of what was going to happen to him at the end of this. There was no stopping this now when the momentum was carrying him ever forward into new territory, but that didn't mean he wasn't going to get hurt somewhere along the line.

There were reasons he didn't get close to people and falling in love was probably the worst thing he could've done. It made him weak, susceptible to more heartache. Before going to the army he'd been too young to get serious with a girl, too single-minded about his career. After his retirement the layers of guilt and self-pity had been too dense for anyone to fight through them to reach his heart. Somehow Emily had found a path straight to that vulnerable spot and it was too late to plug that hole in his defences now.

He'd spent too long running from any form of affection, pre-empting the possibility when there was a chance he'd have his insides ripped apart again. The woman he loved was giving herself to him and now there was nowhere left to run. No reason to run. Any other man wouldn't think twice about letting this play out and enjoy this experience, instead of fearing it. He wanted to be that man, for himself and for Emily, and listen to his heart instead of his head for once. They both deserved a bit of honesty in their feelings for each other, even if they couldn't find the words to express it. He would deal with the consequences later. They couldn't be any more painful than ending this here and not knowing what they could've had. Even for the briefest time.

He could feel goosebumps on her skin under his fingers; the hard points of her nipples pressing against his chest. There was no denying she was as turned on as he was but she was still tense. It was his job, his pleasure to help her relax and enjoy this time with him.

He already knew how responsive she was to his touch so he cupped her breast in his hand and rolled her tight nipple between his finger and thumb. Her gasp of pleasure strengthened his resolve, and his erection. Soon they'd be so consumed with need and lust that nothing else would matter except coming together, and that's exactly how he wanted it.

He wrapped his lips around that sensitive pink nub, teased her with the tip of his tongue to claim his breathy reward. She clung to his shoulders, her nails digging further into his skin with every lap of his tongue. The sharp pain was worth it to see the ecstasy on her face and feel the tension leave her body. It was addictive.

He slid his hand down between her legs and into her wet heat. She was ready for him, her body trembling from need now with every stroke.

'What about protection?' Emily gasped as he lowered her to the floor.

Joe scrabbled for his shorts and pulled a condom from his pocket.

'I always carry one. They're an essential part of a survival kit. You can use them for carrying water and keeping tinder dry.' He didn't want her to think sex was nothing special to him, something he took for granted. Tonight it was everything.

'I think we should probably go down the traditional route and use them as they were intended.' She giggled and took the packet from him to rip it open.

Joe sheathed himself and settled himself between her thighs, slightly nervous himself now since they'd been building toward this moment for so long. Emily lifted her head and kissed him, bringing him back down to the ground with her. Sliding into her, forging their two bodies together was the most natural thing in the world. Nothing was ever going to come close to replacing this feeling of complete happiness. Part of him didn't think he deserved it, while another part never wanted it to end.

He moved slowly inside her, each second of her tight heat a gift he intended to treasure.

He loved her. He couldn't have her. The unfairness of it all drove him to find his peace, every thrust inside her bringing him closer to finding it. She was his sanctuary and he wanted to be hers too. Her body rocked against his, rising and falling in perfect time with him, climbing towards that peak. Every bite of her lip, every moan, every clench and release of her internal muscles charted her journey and Joe wanted to be the one to help her reach that final destination. He braced himself on the cold, hard floor, not caring about anything except watching that bliss play out over her features, and slammed into her again. Emily cried out, clutched him closer and he felt her break apart beneath him. Only then did he give in to his own climax, the primal roar of his release echoing around the walls.

There was a lump in his throat as he looked down at Emily, so beautifully serene beneath him. If he were a different person, in a different life, they could've had this every day. Instead, all they had was until the end of this storm. For both their sakes there was no choice but to let his love die with the embers of the fire. Forever wasn't an option.

Emily lay quietly while Joe spooned in behind her, afraid to speak in case she burst into tears and ruined the mood. This was a monumental moment for her, though she hadn't realised until just now. She had finally moved on from Greg, from her marriage, in the most spectacular fashion—by giving herself completely to someone else. She'd held nothing back here with Joe and perhaps for the first time in her life had truly been at peace, with herself, with him and with what they were doing. Hidden away here, they no longer had to be concerned about outside influences. For this snapshot in time they were able to be true to themselves and each other. When insecurities and obstacles were stripped away they were simply two people who had a very special connection. One that had sparked to life and delivered more than she'd ever dreamed of.

This had been more than sex, even though that was all it ever *could* be. It didn't matter how great they were together or how they felt about each other because it wasn't going to last. This was probably the last time she would ever feel complete happiness because when this was over she'd have to return to her world of playing it safe. It was the only way she could survive.

Joe snuggled into her neck, his warmth reminding her he was still hers for now. She closed her eyes and clung to the thick forearm wrapped around her waist. It wouldn't do any harm to let the fantasy go on a little longer. After all, she was good at this pretending lark.

Emily was jolted from a peaceful slumber by a shout and Joe thrashing on the ground beside her. He tossed and turned, mumbling incoherently as he battled some unknown force in his sleep. She couldn't see his face as it was dark outside and the fire barely more than a glow. It was chilly now they didn't have the heat of passion keeping them warm.

She pulled on her now dry clothes and knelt to add more kindling to the fire. A smile played on her lips as she hugged her knees, watching the embers catch and resurrect the flames. It was representative of what Joe had done for her—taking her dying heart and sparking it back to life. She knew he felt it too, and she'd be lying if she said she wasn't hoping they could do this again. Okay, a long-term relationship might not be viable, given his lifestyle, but he was a traveller and there was no reason he couldn't add England to his list of places to visit. Right now hooking up a couple of times a year seemed preferable to never having this again.

Another flash of lightning illuminated the cave, the crack of thunder ripping through the air after it. Joe was sitting upright, naked, panting and sweating. He was staring off into the distance almost in a trance, his face a mask of utter terror. This was more than a nightmare, he was living this horror right here and now. She moved slowly to his side and rested her hand on his arm, his skin clammy beneath her touch.

'Joe? It's all right. You're here with me.' She tried not to spook him but gently coax him back into the present.

He turned his head slowly towards her but he wasn't really focusing.

'It's me, Emily.' She took a risk by pressing her lips to his. In his current agitated state there was a possibility he'd lash out but she hoped the bond they had was special enough to bring him back to her.

It took a few seconds but he did finally respond, kissing her with a hunger that could only come from the Joe she knew.

'How come you're dressed?' he asked, apparently now wide awake and aware of his surroundings.

'It got cold and look how late it is.' She handed him his own clothes, pity though it was to have him cover up.

'I guess we're here for the night.'

The storm had struck again and Emily saw him flinch, the sight and sounds clearly part of whatever was bothering him.

'That was some bad dream you were having. I was getting worried I wouldn't be able to pull you out of it.'

'I didn't hurt you, did I?' The scowl on his face was more out of concern for her than himself and she guessed this wasn't the first time it had happened.

'No. A lot of shouting and tossing and turning but you didn't lash out.'

'Good.' That seemed enough reassurance for him but that sort of sleep disruption shouldn't be taken lightly. He could do himself serious damage in that trance state in an unfamiliar place, not to mention the exhaustion and lack of concentration that could result from lack of proper sleep—two things that could impair his judgement when it came to treating his own patients.

'Does it happen a lot?' It was in her nature to be inquisitive when it came to people's well-being and Joe was no exception, regardless of his reluctance to talk about it. Doctors often made the worst patients, refusing to accept they were human and fallible just like everyone else.

'Every now and then.' He pulled on his T-shirt so she wasn't able to read his expression. She guessed it happened more than he was prepared to admit since he'd been so quick to move into the clinic on his own.

'Afghanistan?' She took a stab in the dark. By all accounts from her parents it had taken Peter some time to readjust after everything he'd witnessed out there, along with medication, counselling and his faith. Things she was pretty sure Joe hadn't availed himself of since leaving the army. He was too stubborn and tirelessly independent to turn to anyone for help.

'There are a few things that can take me back there in a heartbeat. The senses get a little messed up after being on high alert for so long. One loud bang, a flash of light and I'm back in that tank, helpless, powerless. The mind can play cruel tricks on you when you least expect it.'

'But it's over. I know what happened must've been terrible for all of you but that life is in the past. You still have a future.' With or without her. As long as he was running away from dealing with this he was never going to have the life he deserved—in one place surrounded by people who loved him.

'Batesy and Ste don't. I was the medic, the one who was supposed to be there to save them. I failed to do the one thing I was trained to do. It's my fault they're not here today with their families. How can I expect anyone to rely on me when I can't even trust myself to do the right thing? I mean, the chief's son is lying sick back on Yasi and I'm here, carrying on as if we're on a dirty weekend away.' He wasn't looking at her any more but was staring out at somewhere beyond the ever-changing skies, caught between the past and the present.

Emily knew the rage was directed at himself, fuelled by guilt and grief, but she still took a hit. This was more to her than sex and she certainly would never have intentionally put a patient in jeopardy just to spend some time with Joe. Even if she'd had an inkling of how phenomenal it would be.

'You were injured, you couldn't help what happened to your friends. The only ones to blame are those who planted the bomb. You can't spend the rest of your life afraid of getting close to people in case you let them down. What kind of tribute is that to those who aren't here any more? Taking risks and experiencing things most of us can only imagine is one thing, but shouldn't you be embracing all aspects of life? Including love?' She swallowed hard, catching herself before she blurted out the three words guaranteed to send him running.

Joe was emotionally stripped bare before her, still reeling from his trauma. She didn't need to add more by revealing her feelings for him. He hadn't asked her to fall for him or promised her anything in return. It wasn't fair to expect anything from him now and she knew if she told him she loved him he would feel under pressure to act on it. That's the type of man he was. One who always wanted to do right by others, even if it cost him peace of mind.

There was no way she wanted to increase his burden now she knew that happy-go-lucky façade was hiding his true pain from the rest of the world. Telling him now would only be for selfish reasons, voicing that small hope he would reciprocate her feelings, while all the while knowing nothing could come of it anyway. He'd spelled out the very reasons he couldn't be with her, even if by some miracle he thought of her as more than a holiday romance.

Like her, he was damaged goods. She knew how it was to fake a smile when you were crying on the inside and it was good for him to finally be honest about what he was still going through. The day she'd revealed her birthmark to him had lifted the stress of keeping her secret from her. She hoped this breakthrough tonight would do the same for him in some way. It had taken a great deal of trust from him to confide in her as much as he had, and she was privileged she was getting to know the *real* Joe Braden.

His eyes shimmered in the darkness but he was still refusing to give in to the grief he was obviously suffering. Instead, he ended the conversation by moving in for another kiss. Emily knew he was avoiding further discussion on the subject but she was powerless to resist him when this could be their last opportunity to be together.

They lunged at each other with the urgency of two lovers soon to be separated, possibly for ever.

This time the slow burn of passion was replaced with a fierce need to block out reality and get back to that place of utter contentment as soon as possible when they were both struggling to keep it together. They tore at each other's clothes in their need for a hit of those feel-good endorphins only hot sex could provide. Clinging to each other as though they were adrift at sea, holding on to one another for survival, they joined together in one frantic thrust. For a moment that was all Emily needed, to know he wanted her, that they were together. Then he was moving inside her, turning her thoughts to more primitive needs and how quickly he could take her back to that pinnacle of utter bliss.

Her mind and body were completely consumed by the frenetic pace of their lovemaking as Joe drove into her again and again, chasing away his own demons. There was a moment when their eyes locked, that connection stronger than ever, knowing they both needed this release to free them from their inner turmoil. They came together, their combined cries drowning out the sound of thunder in the distance.

Emily had never known such pleasure and pain, knowing this was the only time they'd have this freedom together. A true passion she'd probably never experience again.

They lay in each other's arms, watching the flames dance in the corner of the cave until Joe's soft snore broke the comfortable silence as he finally seemed to find some peace.

Emily turned on her side and whispered, 'I love you,' safe in the knowledge he wouldn't hear her.

She knew it was the last time she'd ever say it.

'It's time to go.' Joe was gently shaking her awake but she didn't want to open her eyes because that meant facing the truth. The dream was over.

He tried again, a little more forcefully this time. 'We need to get moving before they send a search party out for us.'

She groaned like a truculent teenager forced to get out of bed on a school morning. 'Do we have to?'

'Yes.' He dropped a kiss on her nose.

She supposed food and a warm bed were a good incentive. Plus, if he was brave enough to get that close to her morning breath he must really want to be out of here.

Despite fighting his own demons half the night, Joe clearly hadn't put thoughts of his patient out of his mind. Now it was daylight and their return was inevitable, Emily's concern grew too over what might have occurred in their absence. A more in-depth discussion about Joe's past and his thoughts on a future with her could wait until after they'd checked in with Peter and Miriama.

There was a tad more urgency to her movements now she'd stopped thinking only of herself. She got up but there was no bed to make, no post-coital lazy breakfast together or reason to dilly-dally. Joe kicked some dirt over the fire to make sure it was out and then it was time to leave their little love nest.

They made their way back down to the beach to retrieve the boat from where it had been stashed the night before and pulled it to the edge of the water. The sea was calm today, like flat blue glass for them to slip effortlessly across to Yasi; the sky was as calm as the water. It was almost as if yesterday's drama had never happened.

That wasn't what she wanted at all. Last night with Joe had been the best night of her life. They'd connected in every way imaginable and she didn't want to lose that as soon as they stepped off the island. She still had a few days left before she went home and believed that, given time, they could make this something more than a holiday fling. He'd already started to open up to her and she was willing to risk her heart by giving this a shot.

'What's wrong? Are you sad to be leaving?' Joe didn't seem to understand her attachment to this place, which didn't bode well for a budding romance.

Sleeping with Joe had marked a new chapter in her life. It had put an end to her marriage once and for all. The divorce papers had made it official, but it hadn't been until she'd fallen in love with another man that it had become real to her. She would remember this island for ever as the place where she'd become Emily Jackson again, a single woman living her own life, making her own decisions. She kind of hoped it—she—meant as much to Joe.

He was waiting for her to answer and she thought about laughing it off, pretend last night had been nothing more than sex. But she'd spent too much of her life lying about who she was. If he couldn't handle her feelings, well, she'd simply have to live with the repercussions.

'I don't want this to end. Once we go back to Yasi we're doctors, somebody's family, somebody's friend. Here we're just Emily and Joe, with no expectations from anyone other than ourselves.' A night with Joe had exceeded any expectations she might have had and given her a taste of something special. It wasn't something she was in any hurry to abandon in favour of cool reality. Yasi now seemed like the first step back towards her actual life, where there was no hunky man to spoon with her at night and a whole lot more besides.

With his hands on his hips, his gaze cast down at the

waves washing in and out on the sand, Joe let out a heavy sigh. For a moment Emily worried he might jump in the boat and sail off into the blue without her. Instead, he splashed along the water's edge towards her and wrapped his arms around her waist.

'This won't end until we're both ready.' His words didn't bring her as much comfort as he probably intended because he was still stamping their relationship with a use-by date. It *was* going to end, albeit on a different island with more than swaying palm trees to witness her eventual heartbreak. This might be the new Emily but she still had the same old soft heart. Tears burned the back of her eyelids as Joe gave her one last castaway kiss. She doubted she'd ever be ready. No matter how much notice she had, when the end came it was going to come hard and fast. Joe had left a mark on her soul that wasn't likely to fade any time soon. She knew she'd be thinking of him every time she stepped into the sun.

Joe's head was scrambled, his troubling memories of Afghanistan mixed with those of last night and Emily comforting him. Loving him. He'd spent so long battling the nightmares on his own that he didn't know how to cope with sharing them. Nothing made sense to him any more except kissing her. In some ways he could understand her reluctance to leave. It was easier to stay here wrapped up in each other's arms and ignore everything else outside this slice of paradise. Except hiding wouldn't solve anyone's problems, his least of all.

Even if they chose to push the boat out into the ocean minus its passengers and purposefully strand themselves on this island for ever, it still wouldn't help him reconcile with his faults, or make him the right man for Emily. If something happened out here she'd be dependent on him and that was too much to contemplate for someone who couldn't be trusted with that level of responsibility. Someone who didn't want that level of responsibility again after losing two people he'd loved who were supposedly under his care. Last night, making love to Emily with complete abandon for the first time since leaving the army, had been wonderful but their status couldn't be any more permanent than his stay on this island. As much as he loved her and had probably been searching for her all his life, his wants and needs would have to come second to hers. She deserved more than him.

'Ready?' he said with a forced laugh, making a joke of his last comment before Emily read too much into it. She'd been let down too often. There was no point in leading her on with false promises into believing any of this was real. They had no chance of being together and living happily ever after. That was for heroes, strong men who'd given everything of themselves for others, not those who'd failed in their duty.

'Okay.' Her smile was as fake as his attempt at humour but at least she seemed to understand this need to stop lying to themselves. They had to go back and pick up the reins at the clinic again. It was their job, their calling, their reason for being out here, and it wouldn't do them any good to get too caught up in this fantasy when people depended on them.

As he pushed the boat into the water with Emily on board it was all he could do to jump in beside her, knowing they were sailing towards the end of this romance. The sands of time were shifting ever faster as the sea breeze carried them closer to Yasi and further away from their own personal love island—the only place they could ever truly be together.

When they came ashore on Yasi there was no singing, dancing welcome party to greet them. On the plus side, there wasn't an angry stepbrother waiting for him with a shotgun either. It was going to be pretty obvious what had happened between them left alone on that island all this time when they'd barely been able to keep their hands off each other in company. Peter had already warned him off hurting Emily and that was another promise he knew he was probably going to break when the thought of leaving was already causing him pain. Although she hadn't spoken the exact words, her every look, every touch said she loved him as much as he loved her.

They hauled the boat up onto the beach, where it could be retrieved later. Depending on what they were going back to, it might be used for another voyage soon. There was no point in dragging this out and causing more suffering. If all was well back at the clinic and the chief's house they should probably quit while they were ahead and cherish the happy memories of their night together rather than wait a week for the tears and recriminations to start.

He strode ahead on their walk back into the village in a scene reminiscent of their first meeting. A different couple would have marched along, not caring who knew what had happened or what came next. He couldn't afford that luxury and neither could Emily, though she didn't know it. It was almost inconceivable to think that a few days after their first meeting his whole world would be upside down and he'd broken every one of his relationship rules because of this woman. If Emily expected a loved-up stroll, hand in hand, making the most of their last minutes alone, she didn't say anything. At least nothing he heard.

He paused at the top of the hill to take a breath and a mental snapshot of the view he'd called home for too long. It gave his walking companion time to catch up.

'You seem in an awful hurry to get back.' She moved directly in front of him so there was no escaping the sound of disappointment in her voice.

'I'm sure it's been a long night for everyone. They'll be wondering what's keeping us with the storm long past and half the morning gone already. It's not fair to make them wait any longer than necessary.' They'd had their fun and now it was time to face the consequences.

'Joe? Is everything all right? Between us, I mean?'

This was his opportunity to tell her the truth. Everything between them was far from all right. It was crazy and messed up and scaring the hell out of him enough to consider getting the next boat off the island. Instead he slung an arm around her shoulders as if she was an old mate seeking reassurance on a trivial matter, not a lover asking him about his feelings for her.

'Sure,' he said, his confidence failing him. Going back into the community with shattered hearts suddenly seemed crueller than letting this play out until he had his bag packed.

'I guess we do need time to acclimatise again, give Peter some warning that we were together before he figures it out for himself.' She gave credence to his explanation, increasing his uneasiness by expanding on it until it became her truth. This trust in him was exactly the reason he should leave. He couldn't live up to her expectations and when the blinkers came off it would be in the most humiliating fashion.

'Right,' he said, picking up the pace and carrying the lie away with him.

'The wanderers have returned!' Peter and Miriama were every bit as exhausted and pleased to see them as he'd expected. The guilt slammed into Joe's chest harder than the group hug in which he and Emily were swamped.

'Sorry you had to hold down the fort for so long but we thought it best to wait out the storm.' He immediately felt the need to justify their long delay, even though the reason would've been obvious to anyone who'd witnessed Mother Nature's rage last night.

'I'm just glad you didn't get caught up in it. Did you find somewhere to shelter?' Peter rubbed Emily's arm as if he was trying to generate some heat for her even now. It was a reminder she still had someone to turn to, come what may. Her stepbrother was that person, not someone who was already planning to run away before they reached the first hurdle.

'Joe knew somewhere—'

'We found a place up in the rocks out of the rain.' He cut Emily off before she gave Peter the idea he'd somehow pre-planned all of it.

Besides, the cave had been his secret and it wasn't something he wanted to share with anyone but her even now. Revealing its whereabouts, leaving it open to future visitors, would defile the time they'd spent there together. He wanted them to be the last two inhabitants; the ghosts of their pasts and never-to-be-had future doomed to haunt the stony cavern for ever.

'Good. I had enough to worry about here and figured years of survival training would see you right. Although I would've thought a desert island in a tropical storm was a doddle compared to rain-soaked ditches in the English countryside.'

'You bet. I hope you didn't have too tough a night here without us.' He'd spent the night cuddled up with the most beautiful woman in the world while her stepbrother had been doing the job *he* was supposed to be doing.

'All the delights you'd expect but nothing we couldn't handle. He seems to be through the worst of it for real this time.'

'Thanks, mate. I really appreciate you stepping up to the plate for me. I'm just sorry we put you in that position in the first place.'

'I would say you shouldn't make a habit of it but I reckon we can spare you another couple of hours if you want to have a kip or get changed.'

'That would be great. Cheers.' All of a sudden Peter's generosity made Joe want that space all the more. So no one had died this time, but he had still let his friends down. He could've said no to going in the first place and saved everyone a lot of trouble. He could've insisted on leaving the island at the same time as the others or come back sooner. It had been his selfish wish to spend some alone time with Emily that had put so many people in jeopardy. Pure luck had kept them all from serious harm during his negligence.

He was distracted and unfocused, everything he'd feared would happen if he forged relationships with people. If he hung around here much longer the worst was bound to happen. There was always going to be dengue fever, diabetes, choking babies and people relying on him to save them. Without a local hospital or access to crucial medication the people he'd grown to love were someday going to need more than he could give them. He'd barely come out the other side of grief the last time and he couldn't face it again. He couldn't face these people again knowing he'd failed them. His heart wouldn't survive losing Emily if he failed her too. He'd had a lucky escape this time and it was time to check out while the going was good.

He took off out the door without a backward glance for Emily, afraid that if he looked at her he'd bottle out of this altogether.

'Hey, wait for me.' She'd really got this ninja frontal attack down pat. He didn't even know she was following him until she was there blocking his path.

'Look, Emily, I need some time on my own. Sorry.' He started walking again, unable to offer her a proper explanation when he didn't fully understand why he was throwing this away himself.

'Joe?' Another stealth move and he was faced with those doe eyes pleading with him not to do this.

He had to swallow the ball of emotion lodged in his throat. It was never easy ending a relationship and he was effectively ending two of the most important ones in his life by leaving Yasi. He didn't want to do this out here in the open. Hell, he didn't want to have to do this at all but he was supposed to be a drifter and the difficulty level of ending this was proof he'd already stayed too long.

'I never said I'd be here for ever. Last night proved to me it's time I moved on. I should never have let things get this far and I'm going now before I do any more damage. There are enough of you to carry on what I started. You don't need me any more.' They didn't need him but it was becoming clear that he was starting to lean on them too much and that was equally as dangerous. Spilling his guts to her last night in the wake of his latest nightmare had shown how weak he'd become in getting close to Emily and everyone else on the island. It was only a matter of time before someone got hurt. More hurt.

'I don't suppose the fact I *want* you to stay makes any difference?' She was killing him but this was going to take tough love to make sure she didn't end up mooning after him and ruining the rest of her trip.

'You know I can't stay still. I get bored too easily. I'm grateful for this adventure but, really, I'm ready for the next one.' He saw Emily flinch at his choice of words out of the corner of his eye.

'Joe?' Another plaintive cry for an explanation he couldn't give her.

It broke his heart to ignore it.

'I don't have much to pack so if I can get the chief to agree, I'll be taking the boat out again soon.' He didn't care how he got back to the mainland or how long it took as long as he put some distance between him and Yasi Island fast. It wouldn't take much for his resolve to weaken.

'If that's what you really want...'

'It is.' He was almost gasping for air as the lie choked him. What he wanted was a life with Emily but that was as impossible as Batesy and Ste having theirs back.

'Is that it? You got what you wanted and now you're running out on me?'

'You knew this wasn't for ever. One night together doesn't mean I've changed who I am. I was upfront from the start about my intentions. All I'm doing is putting an end to it sooner than planned. Chalk this up to part of the adventure package.'

He couldn't bear to look at her any more as he stumbled away. Ripping the sticking plaster off with a short, sharp shock was supposed to alleviate the pain more quickly but that expression of betrayal he saw welling up in her eyes was going to stay with him for a long time. He needed to get off this island. Now.

Emily couldn't breathe, the shock of Joe's words sucking the air from her lungs. After last night he knew this was more to her than a holiday fling and she'd hoped he'd felt the same. This sudden coolness and what seemed like unnecessary cruelty was difficult to get her head around when they'd shared so much, grown so close.

Frozen to the spot, all she could do was watch him go. Even the tears she needed to shed for their short-lived relationship refused to fall in her confusion. If she were a stronger person she might have given chase and demanded answers but part of her already knew the answers. He was bored with her. He'd said as much. All of that anxiety she'd felt when Greg had told her the same thing came whooshing back and left her gasping for air. This was reaffirming that idea she wasn't good enough for anyone.

The energy seemed to drain from her body as the implications of his words sank in, leaving her limp and unsteady on her feet. She reached out to brace herself against one of the palm trees that once upon a time had held so many good memories. Now she would always associate everything she loved on this island with this utterly overwhelming sense of desolation. She sank down onto the grass, her body only upright with the support of the solid trunk of the tree. This was how she was going to spend the rest of her days—alone, broken-hearted, unwanted.

Hard-hitting rejection wasn't new to her but it wasn't any less painful the third time around. If anything, it hurt even more than losing her mother or her husband when Joe had appeared so much more supportive and accepting of her for who she was. Last night she'd held him through his night terrors, made love as if they'd been embarking on the start of an exciting journey, and now he was saying it was over? It was hard for her to accept she wasn't anything more to him than any of the other women he'd spent time with on his travels when he'd come to mean so much to her. He was part of her now. He'd helped her learn to love herself again and she'd fallen head over heels for him in the process.

She couldn't imagine going back to her old life as if this had never happened. Neither could she face the rest of her stay here without him. There were memories liable to start a monsoon of tears at every turn. Even from her tragic position here on the ground she could see the hill they'd marched down laden down with her luggage and the school where they'd had so much fun with the children. Her lip began to wobble as she realised this was probably the very tree they'd sat under and shared lunch. If she was expected to forget him she was going to have to leave early too.

She struggled to her feet and resolved to make her way

back to Miriama's before she gave in to the big fat tears
threatening to fall. Once she was behind closed doors
she could mourn properly—cry, rage and eventually decide where to go from here. Whatever happened next was
entirely down to her. From now on she was on her own.

Emily had spent more than enough time moping in her
room like an angsty adolescent. Her throat was raw from
sobbing, her eyes puffy and red from crying, but she knew
she still had to face up to her responsibilities. Just because
her life was falling apart it didn't mean she should neglect
the inhabitants of Yasi. With Joe gone she was the only
doctor left in residence.

    She splashed her face with cold water and pulled her
hair up into a ponytail. There were always going to be patients to treat and her job was the one constant in her life.
At least she was always going to be in demand profession-
ally, if not romantically. In some ways she felt sorry for
Joe. The transient life he led to ensure he didn't get close
to people also meant he never got to fully experience that
feeling of belonging.

    With her mind clearer now the initial shock of his rejec-
tion had passed, she began to analyse that last conversation. He'd given her the impression he'd tired of life here,
that she'd bored him. If this had been England and she was
back in her office with nothing to look forward to than a
cup of tea while watching the soaps on TV she'd buy it.
But not when she'd spent the last days throwing herself
into local customs that ordinarily would have terrified her.
She wasn't that same meek divorcee who'd set foot on the
island and she was ticked off he'd made out she was. After
everything he'd told her she began to wonder if it wasn't
his insecurities he was running away from. He'd been
so locked into his grief and guilt he'd become a martyr
to it, denying himself, and her, any chance of happiness.

She found herself veering towards the clinic. If she didn't try to make sense of this now she knew she'd come to regret it. Whether he was leaving because of her or his own demons, she wanted closure before returning home so she was free to start the next chapter of her life. With or without him.

Her once weak limbs now carried with renewed strength. She'd never taken the opportunity to confront Greg about ending their relationship and had simply walked away with her tail between her legs. Not this time. Good or bad, she wanted honesty about why this was over so she wouldn't be left in limbo.

Unfortunately, by the time she reached the clinic all traces of Joe were gone. All that was left was a scribbled note on the door.

Thanks for everything.
Joe x

That was it? After everything they'd been through together all she deserved was an impersonal message that could've been directed at anyone on the island. She crumpled it in her hand in disgust. He hadn't even managed a proper goodbye to her, to Peter, or anyone else who loved him. She wasn't usually prone to violent outbursts of temper but this all seemed such a waste she wanted to punch things or scream out her frustration.

The hub of the village wasn't the place to do it and she knew she couldn't focus on work until she'd worked through this part of the grieving process. She took the path to the beach instead. The same one Joe would had to have taken to make his escape. She wondered what kind of mindset he'd been in when he'd walked this route. Sad? Relieved? Excited to be starting a new adventure?

Perhaps, instead of spending the last hours weeping

and wailing she should've been finding out. There was a small chance he might even have counted on her coming after him and begging him to stay. After all, she hadn't been honest about the strength of her feelings for him. It was too late to find out if that would have stopped him from leaving.

Her eyes were burning again with those useless tears as she reached the top of the hill. Somewhere in the distance she swore she heard a boat splutter into life. She blinked away the tears to see two figures launching the boat from shore. Joe was there, sailing away for good. This was the last time they'd probably ever see each other and she wanted to make sure there was no way back before she moved on. She raced towards the beach like a woman possessed. He didn't look back, probably because he couldn't hear her yelling over the death rattle of the diesel engine. It was up to her to make him listen.

She kicked off her shoes and didn't think twice before wading out into the water. Joe had taught her not to overthink and complicate matters but to simply jump right in and see where she ended up. Soon the boat would be too far out for her to reach. She gulped in one last breath before diving into the unknown.

Swimming out to a lover who'd jumped on a boat to escape her was either the most romantic gesture ever or the action of a desperate woman who had serious issues about letting go. It was impossible to gauge which way he'd take her action but hopefully he'd spot her soon before she drowned and became some sort of tragic folklore story. She didn't really want to spend eternity wailing for her lost love when she still had a life to get back to at the end of all this.

When she'd expelled all the oxygen in her lungs trying to reach him, she popped her head above the water and waved. The last thing she saw before she sank under the water again was Joe getting to his feet. At least she'd had one final look before she went to her watery grave. That would make the soulful songs about the lonely English-woman who drowned chasing the handsome traveller all the more poignant.

'What the hell are you doing?' Joe was reaching down through the water to grab hold of her. A hero truly wor-thy of becoming part of Yasi folklore.

She climbed into the boat with the help of two pairs of male hands. Excellent, she had a local to regale the rest of the island with tales of her daring escapade. Which was fine if she benefited somehow from this recklessness and didn't make a complete ass of herself. The latter seemed the more likely outcome as she was sitting between two bemused men like a bedraggled mermaid they'd acciden-tally caught in their fishing net.

'I. Thought. You'd. Gone.' Her teeth were chattering with the shock of what she'd just done more than from the cold.

Joe pulled a sweater from his bag and draped it around her shoulders. 'I had to wait until we could take the boat out again. It's stormy out there.'

Only now he'd pointed it out did she realise the skies had clouded over again, matching her unsettled heart.

'I want to know the real reason you're leaving now.'

'You're crazy. *This* is crazy!'

'You drove me to it so the least you can do is be hon-est with me.' It was true in every sense. She'd never have done anything so impulsive before meeting him, never have felt the need if she hadn't have fallen so hard for him.

He stood up, rubbed his hands over his scalp and sat down again. 'I can't believe you did something so stupid.'

'You're the one running away from this when we both know we have something special. In my book that's equally idiotic.'

His sigh came from somewhere deep inside him. Somewhere the truth was probably hiding. 'I told you what happened in Afghanistan. I don't get close, I don't get hurt. Simple.'

He wasn't saying he didn't love her, didn't want to be with her. Reading between the lines, it was because of those reasons he was leaving. Her big brave army doc was afraid to admit to his feelings because of things that might never happen. It was something she could relate to when she'd spent her whole life trying to pre-empt the negative outcome of every situation.

'That's not living. Loving someone, being loved, is part of life. You're the one playing it safe when you know sometimes the biggest risk brings the greatest rewards. What happened to going with the flow? Unless you missed it, things were flowing pretty great until you jumped into this boat and headed out to sea.' A destination that hadn't yet been corrected. If she didn't get through to him soon she'd be making the return journey with only a very tactful islander pretending not to notice her pouring her heart out.

'I don't want you to get hurt.' He took her hand and rubbed the heat back into her fingers, showing he was always tending to her needs without even thinking about it.

'You couldn't hurt me any more than you did by walking out on me without giving us a chance. I want to be with you. Beyond that we'll just see what happens.'

'Damn. You got really bossy in the space of just a few days.' He was smiling as he linked his fingers through hers but she could see the turmoil in his eyes. It was going to be down to her to convince him to take a chance on love. The knowledge he wanted to be with her was powerful enough motivation for her.

'I prefer to think of it as becoming more decisive. I'm taking charge of my life and I want you to be part of it.

I love you, Joe Braden.' Her heart was pounding like a drum as she put it all on the line for him. Joe wasn't the only one taking a risk here. After everything she'd been through, starting a new relationship was like setting foot on Yasi all over again. She had no clue what she was letting herself in for and could only cross her fingers and hope that it would all turn out good in the end.

'And I love this crazy, impulsive Emily. She sounds like the ideal travelling companion for lots of fun new adventures.'

Her heart felt as though it was beating for the first time it was so full of happiness to hear those words and know he meant them.

'So what's the plan from here?' She wanted to go with the momentum, wherever it took them.

'Well, there's a little place I know where we can reconnect and take some time out before we commit to that next step. Perhaps we could take a detour and get our captain to drop us off across the bay before the storm moves in.'

Another shiver rippled up and down Emily's spine, this time with anticipation. It was the ideal place to truly get to know each other and make plans for a future.

One thing was sure, with Joe in her life she'd never be boring again.

EPILOGUE

EMILY WOULD NEVER have believed she'd be back on Yasi Island within a year, much less for a wedding. Her wedding. She looked across at Joe, her husband-to-be, so handsome standing barefoot next to her on the beach. They were never going to have a traditional ceremony and had decided to incorporate elements from Fijian culture into their day.

'Dearly beloved, we are gathered here today to join this man and this woman in holy matrimony.' Peter give them both a smile. Having him officiate made this day truly special, as did having the rest of her family here with them. There was quite a crowd assembled on the beach, all dressed in their finery.

Her wedding dress was a simple, white, strapless gown and Joe had gone with his white shirt and linen trousers. The festive garlands the islanders had bestowed on them, including the ring of flowers in her hair, brought a bright splash of colour to proceedings. Sou, Miriama, her stepmother, and all the other women from the village wore the traditional dresses made from tapa cloth and decorated with the red clay paint that had brought her and Joe so close that special day. The men, bar her father in his Hawaiian-style shirt, were in full warrior costume—she finally got to see the grass skirts! It was all so exotic and exciting it was no wonder she'd found it so hard to settle back home.

After she and Joe had spent the second week of her trip together almost twenty-four hours a day, it hadn't taken much persuading for him to go back to England with her. They'd tried to make it work there but ultimately she'd been the one craving everything Yasi had brought into her life. The regimented schedule had suddenly become too stifling for her and she'd seen Joe's relief when she'd finally admitted it. They didn't have to box themselves into a suburban life in order to be together and he'd proposed when she'd uttered those very words to him.

It had taken a few months to get their affairs in order but they'd both agreed they wanted their new start to begin where they'd first fallen in love. She was looking forward to spending time with Peter again but they hadn't made definite plans to make the island their permanent home. There was a whole world waiting for them out there.

'I do.' Joe gave his promise to love, honour and comfort her, and Emily did the same in return. They'd been there for each other through so much already, to the point she wasn't even wearing her cover-up for her wedding day and his nightmares were becoming rarer with every passing night they spent in each other's arms.

They exchanged simple gold wedding bands as a token of their pledge of love for one another before her stepbrother pronounced them husband and wife and gave them permission to kiss in front of everyone.

'I've never kissed a married woman before,' Joe said when they finally came up for air.

'Well, make sure it's only *your* wife you're kissing,' she said with a grin to match his. 'Wife' was a title she'd worn before but it no longer defined her. She was still Emily. This ring simply meant she was privileged to be sharing the rest of her life with Joe, and vice versa.

'There's no one else I would want to do this with.' He took her hand and kissed her wedding finger, a sign he was talking about his next great adventure and not just a snog here and there. They were in this together.

As the *vakatara*—the orchestra—struck up their percussion instruments and the *matana*—dancers—assembled to begin the celebrations, Emily counted every one of her blessings. The biggest one of all she was yet to share with her new husband. She rested her hand on her slightly rounded belly. In seven months they would embark on a new chapter of their lives and all the new adventures parenthood would bring them.

* * * * *

If you enjoyed this story, check out these other great reads from Karin Baine

THE DOCTOR'S FORBIDDEN FLING
A KISS TO CHANGE HER LIFE
FRENCH FLING TO FOREVER

All available now!

MILLS & BOON®
Hardback – October 2016

ROMANCE

MILLS & BOON®
Large Print – October 2016

ROMANCE

Wallflower, Widow...Wife!	Ann Lethbridge
Bought for the Greek's Revenge	Lynne Graham
An Heir to Make a Marriage	Abby Green
The Greek's Nine-Month Redemption	Maisey Yates
Expecting a Royal Scandal	Caitlin Crews
Return of the Untamed Billionaire	Carol Marinelli
Signed Over to Santino	Maya Blake
Wedded, Bedded, Betrayed	Michelle Smart
The Greek's Nine-Month Surprise	Jennifer Faye
A Baby to Save Their Marriage	Scarlet Wilson
Stranded with Her Rescuer	Nikki Logan
Expecting the Fellani Heir	Lucy Gordon

HISTORICAL

The Many Sins of Cris de Feaux	Louise Allen
Scandal at the Midsummer Ball	Marguerite Kaye & Bronwyn Scott
Marriage Made in Hope	Sophia James
The Highland Laird's Bride	Nicole Locke
An Unsuitable Duchess	Laurie Benson

MEDICAL

Seduced by the Heart Surgeon	Carol Marinelli
Falling for the Single Dad	Emily Forbes
The Fling That Changed Everything	Alison Roberts
A Child to Open Their Hearts	Marion Lennox
The Greek Doctor's Secret Son	Jennifer Taylor
Caught in a Storm of Passion	Lucy Ryder

0916 GEN STD LP

MILLS & BOON®
Hardback – November 2016

ROMANCE

MILLS & BOON
Large Print – November 2016

ROMANCE

Di Sione's Innocent Conquest	Carol Marinelli
A Virgin for Vasquez	Cathy Williams
The Billionaire's Ruthless Affair	Miranda Lee
Master of Her Innocence	Chantelle Shaw
Moretti's Marriage Command	Kate Hewitt
The Flaw in Raffaele's Revenge	Annie West
Bought by Her Italian Boss	Dani Collins
Wedded for His Royal Duty	Susan Meier
His Cinderella Heiress	Marion Lennox
The Bridesmaid's Baby Bump	Kandy Shepherd
Bound by the Unborn Baby	Bella Bucannon

HISTORICAL

The Unexpected Marriage of Gabriel Stone	Louise Allen
The Outcast's Redemption	Sarah Mallory
Claiming the Chaperon's Heart	Anne Herries
Commanded by the French Duke	Meriel Fuller
Unbuttoning the Innocent Miss	Bronwyn Scott

MEDICAL

Tempted by Hollywood's Top Doc	Louisa George
Perfect Rivals...	Amy Ruttan
English Rose in the Outback	Lucy Clark
A Family for Chloe	Lucy Clark
The Doctor's Baby Secret	Scarlet Wilson
Married for the Boss's Baby	Susan Carlisle

MILLS & BOON®

Why shop at millsandboon.co.uk?

Each year, thousands of romance readers find their perfect read at millsandboon.co.uk. That's because we're passionate about bringing you the very best romantic fiction. Here are some of the advantages of shopping at www.millsandboon.co.uk:

* **Get new books first**—you'll be able to buy your favourite books one month before they hit the shops

* **Get exclusive discounts**—you'll also be able to buy our specially created monthly collections, with up to 50% off the RRP

* **Find your favourite authors**—latest news, interviews and new releases for all your favourite authors and series on our website, plus ideas for what to try next

* **Join in**—once you've bought your favourite books, don't forget to register with us to rate, review and join in the discussions

Visit **www.millsandboon.co.uk**
for all this and more today!